T0064041

Library of
Mystory

Library of Mystory

Heroald Chern

PARTRIDGE

To order additional copies of this book, contact
Toll Free 800 101 2657 (Singapore)
Toll Free 1 800 81 7340 (Malaysia)
orders.singapore@partridgepublishing.com

www.partridgepublishing.com/singapore

Contents

Once upon a time

here was a prince who just loved to do nothing but play. Prince Jesper was his name and he could play from dawn till dusk and into the night. His royal servants would be at his beck and call, following him around to play whenever he wanted.

Even as he grew older, his love for playing did not wane and before long, he had grown to be of age. As he was the crown prince, it was a tradition that he would announce whom he would choose to marry on his twenty-first birthday.

The king and queen sent word to all the nobles near and far who had daughters of suitable age as potential candidates to be his bride, but alas, the crown prince would not have any of it; he would rather play chess, practise sword fighting or archery, sing and make merry all day than meet prospective wives.

So, the king and queen met the daughters of the nobles themselves. Interestingly, each and every one of them looked just too prim and proper and in fact, all of them seemed perfect! Unfortunately for the girls, the king and queen knew in their royal hearts that that was far from the truth and the girls were most probably only putting a gloss on their behaviour.

Sensing their dilemma, the king's advisor suggested, "Your Royal Majesty, perhaps we should send the crown prince to a nobles' school where he can observe these girls in their day-to-day lives. That way, Prince Jesper will be able to see the girls for who they really are!"

To this, the king raised an eyebrow and began grilling the royal advisor, "The crown prince?! In a school? What about his safety? What if he gets bullied? What if he doesn't enjoy himself there?"

"Now, dear," the queen said calmingly, "that might not be such a bad idea! We did meet in school ourselves, didn't we? Remember those days strolling in the gardens and exploring the school? Ah! Such fond memories..."

"Yes, yes, but something about that university gives me nightmares. I still dream of some dark library with worms all around," the king frightfully recalled.

The queen patted the king's shoulder as a comforting gesture. "Now, dear, we know those are just dreams. You did say the dreams were a constant source of guidance for you on ruling the country, didn't you?"

"Yes, but the dreams were just too real. There was that time when I was found unconscious near the library, remember? What if that happened to our son too? What if..." the king tried to object further but it all fell on deaf ears. Eventually, he showed signs of relent and added, "But well, I don't think we'll be able to convince him to go to school when we can't even convince him to come in to meet those girls."

"Just leave that to me," the queen said confidently.

The queen immediately went to see the prince. She swept regally over the polished marble corridors to the gardens where the prince was wrestling a poor servant, who was of a much smaller build than he was. The servant gave up soon enough.

"Hmph! You're no fun. Can we get the guards?" complained the prince.

"No, Your Royal Highness, the king specifically gave orders that the soldiers and guards are off-limits."

"But you servants are of no challenge!" the prince protested. Just then, he noticed the queen standing by the side and greeted her with a bow.

"Jesper, how would you like to go to school?" the queen offered.

"School? I already have a private tutor at home who's teaching me all I should know. Besides, school sounds boring. I don't want to read and study all day."

"Oh, that's where you're wrong, Jesper. School is an extremely fun place! There'll be many subjects around your age that you can wrestle with; they'd definitely put up a better fight then your servants here," chuckled the queen.

"Really?! Martin," Prince Jesper called and one of the servants instinctively jumped, "take me to school right away!"

The queen tittered and gave a slight grin, "Jesper, we'll arrange for that tomorrow. For today, just try not to break your royal servants' neck; at least not *too* much."

Prince Jesper nodded gleefully like a boy who had found his toys as he watched his mother leave. Then he eagerly turned towards Martin, "Martin, come! Tell me all about the school I'll be going to..."

Going to School

Prince Jesper could not sleep the previous night. All he could think of was what he would play with his schoolmates when he met them. He was the first one out of bed, the first one at the royal table and the first one to the royal carriage that day.

Prince Jesper had often taken the royal carriage out on hunts where his own horse would follow behind until they were at the hunting ground. However he had never felt as full of anticipation as he was feeling then. He had heard all about Wiston University from Martin the previous night, and now that the carriage was moving ever closer in its direction, he could feel the anticipation mounting.

Suddenly, the carriage stopped. The carriage door opened and Martin's face appeared. "Your Royal Highness, if you please?"

Prince Jesper stepped out of the carriage and looked around. The royal advisor, Kaman, was standing beside Martin, but the school was nowhere to be seen. "Where are we?"

"We'll have to walk the rest of the distance or risk having the royal carriage seen by people. Exposing your identity as the successor to the throne will attract unnecessary danger," Kaman explained. "Martin, guard the carriage." Martin bowed in response.

Just then Kaman's attention was drawn to something gleaming on the floor. He shifted his gaze downwards to the princely feet and immediately remarked disapprovingly, "You're not wearing the correct shoes!"

The prince tilted his head downwards and saw what the royal advisor was upset about. "Martin didn't know what shoes I should wear. I always wear my hunting boots when I get on the royal carriage."

"Never mind, we're running late. Those nobles' kids probably have their eyes so far up their noses to notice what you're wearing on your feet anyway," Kaman said as he ushered the prince forward.

It took them quite a while to reach the school gate. Right before the gates, Kaman warned Prince Jesper, "Your Royal Highness, whatever you do, remember that you must NOT, I repeat, NOT, let anyone know that you're the crown prince, not even that you're a prince or from the royal family or..."

"Relax Kaman, I'm old enough to take care of myself," the prince assured.

"We have our men secretly deployed throughout the school that will be looking out for you so..." Kaman explained.

"You mean like that guy?" the prince interrupted, pointing beyond the metal gates to a sturdy-built man, dressed awkwardly in academic robe who was trying hard to blend in.

"Er... maybe... it doesn't matter, just know that you will be well taken care of. I need to leave before anyone sees us together. Head straight to the head master's office, he'll show you around the school," instructed Kaman.

"Alright! Alright! I'll be fine," the prince started gesturing impatiently to Kaman as he made his way in. As he stepped through the gates, the sight that greeted him was as he had anticipated; teenagers about his age were all over the school compound playing games or happily chatting away with their friends.

As Prince Jesper made his way further into the school premises, he realised that he was lost and randomly stopped a male student to ask for directions, "Greetings, my good royal subject, can you walk me to the head master's office?"

"What? Who do you think you are – the crown prince – calling us royal subjects?"

The prince cleared his throat slightly and proclaimed, "Why, it is I, the crown prince, Prince Jesper."

The student looked at him quizzically and walked off, leaving Prince Jesper in a daze. *That's strange, my royal servants would always bow at my feet whenever they see me.*

He decided to try that on a girl instead and got nearly the same response, except she added, "Yes, then I must be the crown princess," before walking off.

Luckily for him, one of those sturdy built man, awkwardly dressed in academic robe, quietly came over to him and pointed him in the right direction.

Prince Jesper was pleased with himself as it seemed he was on the right track all along and the door to the office was just ahead.

"The crown prince is here!" Prince Jesper announced as he barged into the office.

Unfortunately, the man in the office happened to be sipping coffee while reading the morning papers and got a rude shock, which caused him to spill the coffee all over his papers.

The man slowly set himself right – not completely, since some of the coffee had stained his cuffs – before looking up at Prince Jesper with a menacing look. When he finally spoke, his words seemed to come with a chill, "Yes, Prince Jesper. I was told to expect you. I am your head master and since you'll be studying in MY SCHOOL, I suggest you address me as Sir or Head Master."

He paused as if waiting for the prince to say something. Prince Jesper, not sure of what he should do, muttered, "Yes... err... Sir?"

"Good. Now, you probably know that this is a school for nobles, so the last thing I need is another snobby spoilt brat coming in here, thinking that he owns the world."

There was a long pause. The prince felt rather uncomfortable not knowing what to do. He decided it was best to ask the burning question in his mind there and then, "So, when is playtime?"

The head master looked at the prince with his lips contorted and eyes widened as if the prince had asked him the most incredulous thing in the world. He seemed to consider it for a moment, then shook off that expression and answered with poise, "You'll know soon enough. Now let me bring you to your class."

Meeting the Class

he walk down the hallway was filled with suspense, mainly because the head master just kept walking while the prince just quietly marched along. The bell at the clock tower had just chimed and he could see all the students heading for their classes.

He was too engrossed in looking at everything around him that he did not see the head master stop suddenly in his tracks in front of him. Prince Jesper crashed right into the head master's back and fell back on the floor. He quickly gathered himself and stood up elegantly, "Don't worry, I'm all good."

The head master shot him a look that seemed to say that he did not care, before saying in a hush tone, "I was instructed to remind you that you should not reveal to anyone your identity, but judging from how you made your entrance into my office, you probably couldn't really care less..."

Prince Jesper gave a sheepish smile and a meek chuckle as if in admission.

"I shall introduce you to the class as Vincent, a nobleman's son from a nearby kingdom," the head master said.

"Why can't I just tell people I'm the crown prince, Prince Jesper?" asked the prince.

The head master shot him one of those 'what-kind-of-a-stupid-question-is-that' look and said, "Because THAT, will bring you unwanted attention. Now come."

The head master tapped lightly on the classroom door. Opening it was a shabby-looking bespectacled man whom the head master addressed as Professor Lehrer. They started whispering to each other while stealing occasional glances at the prince. Soon, they seemed to come to an understanding as they broke out of their huddle, shook hands and smiled.

Prince Jesper was amused; he did not think that the head master could smile, which made Prince Jesper smile along. However, as soon as the head master turned to face him, the smile on the old man's face disappeared.

The head master ushered the prince in the direction of Professor Lehrer, who led him into class and introduced him as Vincent.

The prince decided to play along and gave a masculine pose as he added, "Yes, the GREAT and IN-VIN-CI-BLE Vincent!"

Nearly everyone rolled their eyes, except for someone at the back of the class who clapped and cheered.

Prince Jesper was so used to having a big fanfare welcoming his arrival that the lacklustre response by his new classmates greatly disappointed him. *I'm sure if they knew I was the crown prince, it would all be different.* Nonetheless, he was still optimistic that there would be loads of fun things to play in school.

Professor Lehrer directed him to sit at the back of the class where the only available seat was and continued with his lesson.

Professor Lehrer was going through the history of their kingdom, Marvelland. According to him, Marvelland started off as a small kingdom but expanded over the decades through marriages and a series of conquests. In fact, all the kings and queens of Marvelland were all graduates of this Wiston University.

The prince was rather surprised by this new piece of information and so he exclaimed, "I didn't know Father and Mother were from this school!" No sooner had he said those words than he regretted saying them and immediately covered his mouth with his palms in amends.

The whole class gave a puzzled look. That same voice at the back of the class that cheered when Prince Jesper came in shouted, "He must be the crown prince in disguise! Look at his boots!"

That brought everyone's attention to his royal hunting boots. It had the royal symbol on it that only people of the royal family were allowed to have on their attire.

One of the girls immediately got up and went over to him while batting her eyelids, "Hi, I'm Evalia. Are you really Prince Jesper?"

To that, the prince did not know how to respond. Before he could do anything, another girl came forward, fighting for his attention. "I'm Jalena."

Soon, all the girls in the class were fighting for his attention; all except one. She was a red-headed girl in spectacles who sat at the back of the class; the same girl who had cheered Prince Jesper's entrance and given him away.

Finally Professor Lehrer could stand it no more and ordered everyone to get back to their places. The girls all went back to their seats as they stole glances at Prince Jesper. It was then that the prince noticed a different expression on the boys' faces from when he first came into the class; they looked jealous, annoyed and disgusted all at the same time!

Playtime!

t was recess time. Prince Jesper was led out of the classroom towards the dining room by his entourage.

The people around the school were having a word in one another's ears as they looked on at him and his followers, wondering what the commotion was all about.

"Now Prince Jesper, you sit right here, while I get some food for you," a sweet girl, whom Prince Jesper remembered as Madelief, said.

Evalia took this chance to inch closer to the prince. "You know, I'm the reigning beauty queen of this school, so I'm kind of really popular."

The prince took a closer look at Evalia and true enough, she was stunningly beautiful; she had long blonde hair, well-defined features and a beautiful smile.

"Right, whoever gave you THAT title?" said another girl, Jalena, who was equally as beautiful, but in a different way. Her wavy black hair complemented her big round eyes and smooth jawline.

Prince Jesper was enjoying school already as he liked all the attention that he got. Then, something caught his eye: the red-headed girl who sat at the back of the class, seemingly impervious to his charm, was sitting at a table, reading a book and eating her lunch alone.

"Who is that girl?" Jesper pointed to her.

"Oh, she? She's Ida. She's just a nobody, not even of noble status," Evalia explained disdainfully.

Prince Jesper looked confused. "Then why is she studying in this school? Isn't this a school for nobles?"

"She is Professor Lehrer's daughter. The head master lets her stay in the class so long as she doesn't give anyone any trouble," Evalia said with the same look of disdain.

Suddenly, a loud "bang" on the table broke up the conversation.

"Hey, prince!" It was one of the boys from his class.

Jalena stood up and said, "What do you want, Kegan Junker? Can't you see that the prince is busy?"

"Now prince, I heard you're pretty good at sports. Would you like to join us in a game of football?" Kegan said, almost tauntingly.

The moment he heard the word 'game', Prince Jesper's eyes lit up with enthusiasm. "Yes!" He got up eagerly to leave with Kegan. The girls had no choice but to follow suit.

Of course, when Madelief came back with two servings of lunch, she was wondering where everyone had gone!

Prince Jesper was all excited about the game. He played football occasionally with the royal servants and much to his pride, whichever team that he was on would always end up being the winner.

They reached the field and Kegan gave Prince Jesper a haughty look. "This will be our playing field. First to three goals wins. Are you aware of the rules of the game or do I have to explain them to you?"

Prince Jesper just nodded his head profusely like a puppy hungry for food. "So, who's going to be on my team?"

"Oh, we've already got ourselves a team. *You* can probably get those guys over there as your teammates." Kegan pointed to a bunch of scrawny looking guys seated at the side of the field who looked eager to join the game.

Prince Jesper gave a frown as he considered them for a while. At that, Kegan's smirk widened as he looked around at his peers vaingloriously.

After a while, Prince Jesper began to smile and nod. "They're perfect! They look just like my royal servants! Let's get the game started!"

It was Kegan's turn to frown. Prince Jesper did not waste any time and gathered his teammates to give some last minute instructions. Not to be outdone, Kegan immediately did the same.

The girls moved themselves to the sideline and started cheering for the prince who had moved to the center of the field after the huddle to meet Kegan.

"Oh almighty prince, I shall let you choose whether to start first or choose your starting goal post," announced Kegan mockingly.

"I shall start first," the prince eagerly declared.

Evalia, who happened to be standing beside the leather ball, threw it to Prince Jesper from the side. With a confident wink at her, the prince was off, dribbling the ball past a first defender and approaching the next.

Kegan was not one to be beaten so he sprinted up and made a hard tackle for the ball, sending the ball out of bounds and the prince spread-eagled on the floor.

The opposing team snorted in laughter as they pointed at the prince.

"Hey, that's a foul!" screamed Jalena from the side. From another corner, one of the burly-sized "professors" began to react.

"Oh, I'm sorry; I didn't know the prince was THAT weak!" Kegan responded mockingly, to which his cronies laughed even louder.

Just as his supporters and teammates were about to rush over to him, Prince Jesper abruptly raised his hand to stop everyone in their tracks. He slowly made his way up and to the surprise of everyone there, there was a wide grin across his face!

Even though Prince Jesper was taken aback to be manhandled, he was more thrilled to finally have competitors worthy of a challenge!

"Two can play that game! Team, let's PLAY BALL!" cried the prince.

Before Kegan could react, Prince Jesper had run over to the sideline to inbound the ball by throwing it off the head of one of his opponents. The prince ran forward, shoving Kegan along the way, to catch the rebounding ball with his feet.

With a series of spectacular dribbles, the prince passed the remaining defenders and scored the first goal. This won thunderous applause from the crowd.

Prince Jesper did a celebratory bow to the crowd and saw the red-headed girl amongst them while Kegan gave a growl to show his displeasure.

The game raged on with twice the intensity, but the prince's speed and skill were unparalleled. With sensational moves on full display, it was not long before the teenager made three goals.

He was carried by his teammates and cheered off the field. Before leaving, Evalia made a mocking gesture to Kegan with her thumb on her nose and her tongue sticking out.

Kegan looked on in fury; he clenched his fist and gave a look that vowed revenge.

Into the Library

da was reading her books in the library like she always did after school. All of a sudden, her father rushed out of the library storeroom and hastily passed her two items: a badge and a pen.

"What's all these?" asked a puzzled Ida as she examined the items in her hands.

"Hold on to them for me. I've got something important to attend to. Keep them safe," and with the same urgency, he left the library, leaving Ida to wonder what was going on.

The school library was usually very quiet. Rich children did not need the school library, mostly because they had more than enough books in their personal library at home or they were more into enjoying life than studying.

With a shrug, Ida sat back on the floor and continued with her reading. Shortly after, Prince Jesper ran into the library in a frantic manner. His entrance distracted Ida who asked, "Prince Jesper. What brings you here?"

"Please, quick, I need a place to hide!" came the distressed reply.

"Oh, I see. Those girls being too much of a handful for you?" teased Ida.

"No time to lose, your father said to hide in the storeroom. Where is it?"

"Wait? My father?" but the prince was not listening; he was heading for the room that had a sign 'Keep Out! Authorised Personnel Only!'

"Hey stop! Where are you going?" demanded Ida, who started to stand.

"I'm looking for the storeroom and this is the only room in this library so I'm guessing this must be it," the prince said with his hands almost to the door knob.

"Stop! Can't you read?" Ida said as she intercepted the prince and stood between him and the door.

"Um... well, I just don't know *some* of the words..." the prince confessed.

"It says 'Authorised Personnel Only'," Ida said as she pushed the prince backwards with both her hands; she felt it was her duty to protect the library while her father was not around. After all, her father was a professor in the school and the resident librarian.

"Well, I'm the crown prince, so I should be 'Authorised' enough, and besides, your father told me to hide here." In two shakes of a lamb's tail, the prince had forcefully pushed Ida aside, opened the door and gone into the room.

Ida had no choice but to chase after him. Even though she had been to the library very often, it was the first time she had entered the storeroom.

"Quick, close the door. They'll be here any second!" the prince said hurriedly.

Looking at how he was behaving, Ida knew that there was more to the story. "What really happened?"

"Well, it's as you guessed; the girls are really getting on my nerves. Each one was just trying to outdo the other to get my attention. A few days ago, when I first came, that was still fine. Now, it is really starting to get irritating! But that's not all, the boys in the school are getting jealous of the attention I'm getting and I have been chased around by almost everyone!" the prince said confoundedly.

"I heard you love games. Isn't this like a game to you where you see how many girls' hearts you can break?" Ida bantered.

"What? No! I would never do that! And besides, I would rather spend more time horse riding than waste time womanising!" said the prince indignantly.

All of a sudden, noise could be heard coming from the other side of the door.

"Oh no, they're here in the library! They're bound to open this door and find me standing right here!" the prince said in a frantic whisper. He began to anxiously look for another exit.

"What's this?" He pulled aside a curtain and unveiled a wall with a painting of a door on it. Above the painted door arch were the words 'Library of Mystory'.

"Somebody must have painted this and misspelt 'Mystery'. It looks like a very old wall mural though," Ida said as she began to touch the wall. The moment she did that, the mural lit up as if by a magical spell. The room was filled with the brilliance of the miraculous sight before them. As the light began to dim, the artwork came to life and became a real door!

"What's... going..." before Ida could finish the question, the sound of footsteps in the library drew nearer the storeroom door.

The prince panicked and said, "No time to think about that! Quick! Let's go in! And draw the curtain behind you!"

He opened the magical door and dragged Ida by the hand through it, then used the curtain to conceal the door as he closed the magical door.

"THUMP!" In his anxiety, he closed the magical door a tad too loud. Prince Jesper cringed, wide-eyed with his mouth half-agape, at his foolishness. He leaned back on the door with his right ear squarely on it to listen out for any movements.

For a long time, Ida stared at the prince, feeling his tension, as he leaned there on the door listening.

When no noise came, he finally relaxed. Then, Ida laughed.

"What's so funny?"

"You should have seen your expression just now. It was absolutely hilarious."

"No, it was not!" retorted the prince loudly. Ida immediately placed a finger to her mouth as she stared in horror at the prince for speaking too loud.

He immediately put his ears against the door again to check for any noise from beyond the door, and when he heard none, he heaved a sigh of relief.

Ida laughed quietly to herself this time. She knew that if she laughed any louder, the prince would get offended again.

"Where are we?" the prince's question snapped her out of her muted laughter.

Ida looked around. She was as puzzled as the prince was as to where they were. It was then that Ida noticed that the badge that her father had given her was beaming out a bright ray of light.

"What's that you have there?" Prince Jesper asked curiously.

"My father passed it to me just now. It seems like it's magical." She took it out of her pocket and shone it around.

It seemed like they were in some sort of a library as there were shelves of books lined up neatly in rows. However, the library was rather dark except for a faint glow coming from the other end of the library.

The prince started walking along the aisle in the direction of the glow and Ida hastily followed; she did not want to be left alone in this eerie place. Occasionally, the books on the shelves would radiate an odd orange glow, adding to the spooky feel of the library and when that happened, shreds of paper would mysteriously fly out of the books, as if being coughed up by them.

Ida felt a shiver down her spine as she looked around the massive hall. *It sure is a 'Library of Mystery'*. Then, something caught her eye: an oddly-shaped human-sized silhouette that was among the shelves.

She lightly tugged at Prince Jesper's robe and pointed in that direction. They both tiptoed closer to get a better look as Ida shone her badge towards the figure. It seemed to be arranging the books on the shelves. Then it turned around and ended up facing them when it was done with its work.

Then, the duo and the creature came face-to-face with each other, and all of them screamed in horror; it was a worm!

"Shhhhhhh!" came from all over the library.

The worm immediately straightened itself up and said, "This is a library. Please be quiet."

The both of them immediately covered their mouths as they widened their eyes to stare at the worm which had just spoken.

Ida slowly removed her hands from her mouth and said, "Who are you?"

The worm immediately replied, "I'm the Official Book-Keeper I-J. You may call me I-J."

This was not really the answer she was looking for. She was still trying to come to terms with talking to a worm, "Are you a... a worm?"

I-J replied matter-of-factly, "Why, of course I'm a worm. I'm a bookworm to be exact. What do you expect to find in a library? Grasshoppers?"

Prince Jesper laughed hard as if he had just heard the most ridiculous joke, then covered his mouth again when the "Shhhhhhhh!" came from all corners of the library.

The worm gave Jesper a weird look before saying, "You two must be lost." the worm said.

"No, I must be dreaming," Prince Jesper said, as he started slapping himself on the face hard. "OUCH! It really hurts!"

"And you must be a clown too, with a bad sense of humour," the worm chuckled unamused. Prince Jesper did not seem quite happy at that remark.

Sensing that she had to ease the tension, Ida quickly asked, "Anyway, where are we?" The fact that she was talking to a worm now seemed secondary.

"Well, as the Official Book-Keeper I-J, I'm obliged to tell you that you're in the Library of Mystory. This, you've probably read when you walked in through that door," the worm answered patronisingly.

"Mystory? I thought it was a misspelling of 'Mystery'. What does it mean?" Ida queried.

"It just means 'My. Story.' This is the library where everyone's life story is kept," the worm explained.

"Oh, I get it, 'My-story'. Like the stories of people long ago!" Prince Jesper interjected, sounding rather pleased with himself.

"No, that's the Library of History. Once your book gets old enough it will probably be stored there."

Noticing the glow that occasionally came from some of the books on the shelves, Ida turned to question the worm, "Pardon me for asking, but why are the books emitting light from time to time?"

"When someone's future changes, a green light will emanate from the book and when the future becomes present and gets cast in stone – well, it gets etched in stone, literally – it will glow orange. If you had read your librarian handbook, you would have known that," explained the worm.

"Librarian handbook? Why would I have one of that? I'm not a librarian, you must be mistaken," asked Ida in amusement.

"Why of course you are! You're holding the librarian badge!" I-J stated matter-of-factly while using his face to point at the badge in Ida's hand that her father had given her. This took Ida aback slightly and she began to study the badge intensely.

"I'm sorry; I don't quite understand all these 'librarian' talk. Could you please tell us another way to get out of this creepy library instead?" the prince urged.

"Well I'm afraid the only entrance or exit is through that door you came in by," said the worm as he pointed back the way they came with his tail.

"No way! Arhh...!!" Prince Jesper grunted.

"This is a library, please keep your volume down," demanded the worm.

"Well I'm the prince, I can do whatever..."

As the two of them continued their bickering, Ida noticed that the bookshelves were labelled with different letters and the one she was nearest had a big letter 'J' on the side panel.

Hmmm, I wonder....

What the Books Foretold

da found the bookshelf with the letter 'I' on it.

Eagerly, she began searching for her name among the books. "Ian, Iban, Icarus... there!" There, on the relatively empty bookshelf, was a book with the words 'Ida Lehrer' written on the spine.

Ida fervently made a grab for it and was almost taken by surprise by the weight of the book. The front few pages were made of a stone-like material, while the remaining pages, which made up the bulk of the book, were of paper.

She flipped to the first page and used her badge to shine on it. There, etched in stone yet vivid was a picture of a cute baby girl staring back at her. It was her!

"What are you doing?!" I-J shouted as he wriggled his way over to Ida.

"I'm just...erm," Ida was lost for words.

"Well don't worry about it, you're a librarian, you can do whatever you want here," I-J said with a straight face, but he quickly turned to Prince Jesper and added, "but not you! You're just a nobody here."

That got the prince clenching his fist and teeth as he rushed over to pursue the argument.

Ida was relieved to not have to answer to I-J. She left them to their squabbles and sat down with her book to continue flipping through it.

The stone pages all showed the things that happened in the past while the pages of paper showed Ida doing things that seemed unfamiliar to her.

"What does the pages in paper show?" Ida queried I-J, interrupting Prince Jesper and I-J in their dispute.

"They show their owners' future of course!" I-J said as he wiggled his way back to Ida, leaving Prince Jesper to stand there pouting his lips and crossing his arm. "Though every time their owners decide to do something different in their lives, the books will have to erase away the old entry and write in their new fate!"

"Fate? I don't think I quite believe in fate because I believe we command our own destiny," Ida refuted politely.

"Well then you probably do not understand the concept of fate very well. Fate doesn't mean you have no choice in your destiny, instead it means if you choose to do something, the consequence will almost definitely happen: like if you choose not to sleep early the night before, you're almost definitely going to wake up feeling very tired – cause and effect – fate."

Ida flipped the pages as Prince Jesper inched closer to peep. It showed her listening to I-J's instructions and getting back to the outside world, studying hard and becoming a famous professor like her father. Subsequent pages showed imagery of her leaving the country because of a civil war, growing old and continuing to teach in some other universities.

Prince Jesper looked intrigued, "I want to know my fate too!"

I-J opposed, "No! Only librarians may have access to the library books."

Prince Jesper gave a deep frown and rebutted, "I'm the crown prince and I have access to anything I want!"

"No! I'm under strict orders!" came the firm answer.

Ida knew that both of them were not likely to back down from their stand and quickly stepped in, "I-J, may I please have a look at Prince Jesper's book then?"

Ida's request seemed to have I-J defeated as he was dumbfounded for a moment, looking intensely back and forth between Prince Jesper and Ida. Finally he gave a sigh of resignation and said, "It's over at the 'J' shelf."

Ida already knew where it roughly was from the experience of finding her own so it did not take long for her to locate the book with the spine that read 'Jesper Koenig'. She brought the book down from the shelf and opened it before I-J and Prince Jesper.

Using her light-emitting badge, she shone at the first few stone pages of the book, which illustrated the story of a baby boy born into the royal family. The boy grew to become a playful toddler. The various stone pages showed pictures of him refusing to study and instead whiling his time away.

Then on the first page in paper, there were many moving pictures. The first one seemed to have a slightly different texture around it and showed him coming to Wiston University. The next few pictures were against the normal paper texture. One showed him clowning around in class and refusing to learn to read.

The next picture showed him playing beside the bed of the king who seemed to be very sick. There was aversion written all over the faces of the royal subjects in the room.

The subsequent picture showed him challenging Kegan and triumphing over him. Kegan's face was filled with anger.

On the same page, there was a picture displaying an old lady drowning in the river and Prince Jesper passing by the stream, oblivious to the calls of the helpless old lady.

On the next page, a picture showed Prince Jesper choosing Evalia as his wife.

The next few pages had pictures that showed him dealing with court disputes and country unrest before dying at the hands of Kegan!

When Ida lowered her badge and looked up from the book to analyse Prince Jesper's reactions, she could clearly see he was disturbed by what he saw. She looked at I-J for help but he too seemed lost for words and for the first time, seemed less imperious.

"Is this my future?" Prince Jesper asked, looking at no one in particular but seeming to direct the question at I-J.

I-J seemed to think hard for a moment before choosing his words carefully, "You can't change the things shown on the pages in stone as they have already happened but the pictures on the paper pages are key events that will shape your future. At each of the events there will be a key decision that you will have to make that will cause the rest of your future to change."

"But the pages in paper show..."

"The pages show the likely decision that you will make based on your current character and what you have done. Like I said – 'fate'. You reap what you sow."

"So I just have to remember NOT to make all those decisions that I have just seen and do something else and the disastrous future won't happen, right?" Prince Jesper stated with his lips trembling.

I-J sighed with a faint frown, "Unfortunately, you won't remember a single thing after you leave this library. There is a magical charm in this library that prevents visitors from remembering what they have seen here after they leave this room."

"I-J please, we can't let that happen, he must remember so that he can change his future: OUR country's future!" Ida pleaded.

I-J shook his head and sighed, "I'm sorry Miss Librarian, there's really nothing that I can do. I don't even know any magic; I'm just poor old bookworm I-J. Seriously, you librarians have an odd sense of logic, you created us to help you keep the books in order but won't even give us a pair of hands to move the books or write."

"Write?! That's it! We just got to write it down somewhere for Prince Jesper to bring it home so that he can remember to do those things!"

"That may work, but what are you going to write with? We don't have any pen here. Only the head librarian carries a pen around."

"A pen?" That was when Ida remembered that her father had passed her a pen. She reached into her pockets to take out the pen to examine it. Its tip seemed to have been dipped in ink, but it did not stain her clothes.

Then I-J noticed her holding the pen. "The magical self-inking pen! Why is it with you?" I-J seemed to be overcome with shock but quickly recovered to point out, "No matter. You don't have any paper to write on."

"Of course there is, there are so many books around!" Prince Jesper pointed out.

"NO!! I forbid you to use any paper from anyone else's book! Each page is equivalent to a year of someone's life! Tearing the pages may shorten their lives!" I-J bellowed firmly at Prince Jesper.

With a look of realisation, Ida asked, "Wait, all those pictures in his book were shown to happen within a few pages! Does that mean all those things are going to happen within the next few years?!"

"Yes. The part about him choosing a wife seems to be on his birthday, which starts the new page and it seems shortly after that, he is going to be stabbed," I-J answered stoically.

This made the young lady decide there and then that she had to do something anon. Everyone in the country was going to suffer if the country was to go into civil war and it was going to happen within the year! She could not let that happen.

She picked up her book and turned to the last few pages. *Page eighty-one. It's empty. I don't think I'll live that long so I probably won't need it.*

She was about to tear the page out when I-J noticed what she was doing, "Ms Librarian, you mustn't do this. This is against the rules of our library. Look." I-J used his tail to point to a board on the side wall.

Straining her eyes, Ida pointed the light-emitting badge up at the board and tried to read what was written.

Rule Number 1 No library staff may divulge any information from or about the library to anyone else.

Rule Number 2: No library staff may take any book or part thereof out of the library. Any book removed from the library will cause the death of its owner.

Rule Number 3: No one may damage or destroy any items in this library.

Rule Number 4: No library staff may intentionally change the fate of someone or something having known the outcome from the books in the library.

Rule Number 5: A librarian may bring no more than one guest at a time into the library for the sole purpose of verifying the reliability of the records. A magical charm is in place to remove the guest's memory of the visit once they leave the library.

Rule Number 6: No royalty or person of noble status is allowed to be a librarian.

At the bottom of the board were fine prints that Ida could not make out.

Prince Jesper questioned, "What do the rules say?" This broke Ida's concentration on reading the board.

"Can't you read it yourself?" Ida shot back. Her mind was preoccupied with the dilemma at hand. She was about to break the library's rules. That might get her father into trouble as he was obviously a librarian there but on the other hand, the lives of thousands were at stake.

She bit her lips, took in a deep breath as she closed her eyes. When she opened her eyes again, she had a look of conviction as she started scribbling furiously on her page.

Over her shoulders, I-J and Prince Jesper tried to peep at what she was writing but before they could do that, she was done. She tore the page out from the book, folded it and stuffed it in a pocket on his gown. "This should be the safest and most obvious place to find something. Now Prince Jesper, try very hard to remember to read the note."

"Don't worry about me; I'll definitely remember such a trivial thing. I think the girls are gone by now. Let's get out of here. This place gives me the creeps," Prince Jesper said as he supplemented his words with a shiver.

Ida nodded her head in agreement then turned to I-J to say, "Thank you, I-J, for all your help. Take care and good bye." She felt a strong grasp on her left hand and turned around to find Prince Jesper pulling her by the hand towards the door from which they entered.

Behind her, I-J was trying his best to keep up as he shouted, "Wait! Wait! Bringing any part of the book out of the library is against the rules…." All that seemed to fall on deaf ears as they hastily barged their way out.

Bright lights engulfed them, blinding them.

When they could see again, they found that they were standing in front of the mural. Ida turned back to see the same bright light, which had previously revealed the door to them, now transforming it back into the mural.

She heaved an extended breath out of her lungs then turned to Prince Jesper.

"Remember the important thing in your pocket," she reminded him.

He grinned proudly and boasted, "Something as important as..." but he was unable to finish his sentence. His head seemed to be spinning as he stood unsteadily. He reached for his temple with his right fingers.

Then he fainted.

Has he Gone Mad?

rince Jesper woke up that morning as if he had been asleep for a very long time. He gave a lazy yawn as he tried to sit upright.

Martin, who was keeping watch beside him instantly rose to attention. "Your Royal Highness, you're finally awake! I was so worried for you. I'll send word to the queen immediately."

"What happened?" Prince Jesper asked.

"You don't remember?" Martin paused to look at Prince Jesper as if waiting for some form of recollection from him. When none came, he continued, "Well our secret servants reported that you were chased by a group of girls. You bumped into Professor Lehrer who said something to you and pointed to the school library. You ran in before the group of girls came around the corner and bumped into Professor Lehrer who scolded them for running along the corridors of the school and directed them in another direction."

"I seem to vaguely recall some of that," Prince Jesper acknowledged. "Then why was I lying in bed?"

"The secret servant ran into the library to search for you but you were nowhere to be found. Then, nearly an hour later, a girl in spectacles, pulled you by the underarms out from the storeroom. She said you had fainted in there from all that running. You were out for a few hours!"

"A few hours? It's morning! Does it mean I've missed class?" Prince Jesper asked, almost in disbelief.

"Unfortunately no, today is Saturday and there's no school over the weekends," Martin replied, who seemed to be trying as best as he could to sound like he was disappointed.

"Phew…" Prince Jesper sighed with a look of relief.

"Your Royal Highness, I might be wrong but I seem to detect a sense of gladness that you did not miss a day of school," Martin probed.

"Why of course!"

"But weren't you very troubled by the girls chasing you all around school?"

"Yes maybe but I suddenly have the strong urge to study!"

"Your Royal Highness, I might be wrong but again I could have sworn I heard you say 'to study'!"

"Yes, quick, get me my personal tutor. I want to learn how to read as quickly as I can."

"But it's your play…"

"Now, Martin!" Prince Jesper exclaimed with excitement. For some weird reason, he was feeling a strong need to learn how to read and had a strong detest for playing. He could hear Martin outside the room speaking rather loudly to the page boy, "Oh dear, Prince Jesper must have hurt his head! Quick get the royal doctor! Let the queen know about this! Oh! And get his personal tutor; he asked for him!"

Prince Jesper let out a quiet laugh. He was enjoying this already. Unfortunately, the royal doctor was the first to arrive. The king and queen arrived while he was examining Prince Jesper.

The royal doctor checked his pulse, tested his reflexes and even got him to look at the doctor's finger as he moved it left and right before the prince's eyes. Finally he declared that he found nothing wrong with the prince.

Just then, there was a knock on the door. A head belonging to Prince Jesper's personal tutor popped in between the doors. "I'm very sorry for being late. I was told that I was summoned by the prince himself but I thought the page boy was pulling my leg so I didn't barge until I heard the servants talking about it too."

"Mr Pfaff!" Prince Jesper cheered, sounding rather excited. He got out of bed and chased everyone out of his room except for his tutor, Mr Pfaff. "Now let's get started!"

Outside the room, the king, queen and servants strained their ears to try to listen out for what Prince Jesper and Mr Pfaff were talking about.

The muffled voice of Mr Pfaff teaching Prince Jesper could be faintly heard. It was not long before a look of realisation came all over their faces; Prince Jesper was really studying!

Back Home

da's arms were aching from lugging Prince Jesper out of the storeroom. *Who would have thought a young prince could be so heavy?*

It was way past midnight as Ida massaged both her hands and trudged her way back to her dormitory. Too tired to push with her hands, she thrust the door open with her shoulders. She realised the room was in darkness. *That's weird; Father should be home by now.*

She groped for her light-emitting librarian badge in her pocket and took it out to look around the room. Suddenly, she saw movement in the middle of the room from the corner of her eye and somehow managed to identify the figure to be her father.

"Father!" Ida said, "Why didn't you light the lamps?"

"No! Ida! Don't!"

Ida brought the badge close to Professor Lehrer's face and that was when she noticed something was wrong. "Father! What happened to your face?!"

There was something starkly different about her father's face and the moment she queried her father about it, he bowed over and hid his face behind his hands.

Ida put down the badge on the table and tried frantically to remove his hands in an attempt to get a better look at his face. Eventually Professor Lehrer stopped putting up a fight and Ida was able to slowly peel his hands away from his face with her fingers.

Beneath the veil of flesh was a face Ida could hardly recognise. Her hands followed her gasp to her mouth. She stood dumbfounded and felt a surge of emotions welling up within her.

"Father…" was all Ida could muster.

"Ida, I didn't want you to see me like this. I was trying to write my farewell letter as quickly as I could but the evening came too soon and my hands were not as nimble as it was used to. I couldn't light the lamp nor finish writing the letter before you came back," his voice sounded weary.

"Father, it's ok. I'm not afraid. Just tell me what happened. What made you become like that?"

"Ida, I'm sure you figured out that I'm the Head Librarian of the Library of Mystory. It's an honorary position that was bestowed upon me for my many years of contribution to the university. However, that honour comes with a price. No librarian may divulge anything about or from the library or intentionally change the fate of something or someone, having known the outcome from the book…" Professor Lehrer took a deep breath before sighing, "I broke that rule today… twice."

"I saw the rules on the board, but how did that cause this to happen?" Ida questioned in a stutter, sounding almost as if she was about to cry.

"In fine prints at the bottom of the board detailed the punishment that will be magically meted out should any librarian flout the rules. Each time we break the rules, ten years of our lives will be taken away from us."

"Father…, why did you do it then?"

"I was checking the books as usual when I chanced upon my own book. The future had changed from the last time I saw it and I believed it was because of Prince Jesper's sudden admission into our school. That must have started a chain of events that will eventually result in a horrible civil war that tears our country apart. I cannot let that happen, no matter the sacrifice."

"So that was why you chose to direct Prince Jesper to the library and give me the librarian badge and pen!"

"No... not really. I'm sorry Ida, I was worried that taking ten or twenty years off my life would have taken my life, so I had to make sure someone I could trust sees the whole thing through. I'm sorry Ida, I'm sorry..."

"Father, don't be. I'm glad to be of any help."

"Ida, you don't understand...," Professor Lehrer stopped and brought Ida and the librarian badge to the mirror in Ida's room. "Look!"

The light given off by the badge in her father's hand was shining at an angle which made it difficult for her to see herself without being overly glaring. Thus, she took the badge from her father and adjusted it herself. Ida examined herself carefully in the mirror.

Then she saw it, and she screamed.

Reality Bites

da had been crying the whole morning. When she realised that she had aged by ten years in a day, it had hit her very hard. Her father had explained to her that the role of a librarian could be shared with a family member.

That was why she could enter the library and I-J kept referring to her as the librarian. That was why she could make the magical pen work and because she had torn the page off her own book, she, as the librarian, had knowingly attempted to alter the fate of someone and damaged a book from the library.

She guessed she should thank her lucky stars that somehow the magic of the library only considered all these to be one violation and only punished her once, but that was not what upset her most.

The part that made her cry was that there was no spell or anything that her father knew of that could break the curse.

Her father was now probably the age of sixty-eight and feeling very frail. Years of neglecting his health in favour of his work and the sudden ageing might have contributed to him taking quite a while to get accustomed to his 'new' old body.

As Ida worried about her father, she started to think about herself too. She was now nearly thirty-one and if she were to make sure the country did not fall into despair, she had to see Prince Jesper through turning over a new leaf which could mean a few more multiples of ten years off her life.

She was not sure if she was ready for that. She was not even sure if she was ready for anything. All she wanted to do that day was to lie in bed and cry.

Then she thought of Prince Jesper. She did not hate him but knowing that an entire nation's fate depended on him – or for that matter, on Ida – made her feel pressurized. She tried to recall what the five critical events were.

She recalled that the first picture was about him making a mockery of his class and taking learning lightly. *Could this mean that if Prince Jesper is to have any chance of changing his fate, he must take his education seriously?*

Then the second picture was about the king being sick and Prince Jesper drawing the contempt of his subjects by being indifferent around the king's sick bed. *This must mean that Prince Jesper has to show care and concern to his father while he is ill.*

She recalled a picture to do with Prince Jesper challenging Kegan. *Challenging Kegan will probably make Kegan rebel. After all, Kegan is from a family of nobles with strong backing. He can easily instigate any rebellion he wants.*

There was a picture of Prince Jesper letting an old lady drown. She did not recognise the old lady. *Maybe the old lady is someone influential and her death must have caused even more people to rebel.*

Then there was one last picture of Prince Jesper choosing Evalia as his wife. *Why would that be bad? If anything, they seemed to be made for each other, simply because Evalia was mostly annoying at times and Prince Jesper was mostly silly at times.*

Thinking of Prince Jesper and his antics made Ida give a short titter. But as she thought about it, the joy quickly became frustration. "Why.... Why, why can't I go back to being just 'Invisible Ida' who sits at the back of the class?"

Then a rustling noise from her laundry yesterday startled her, with a familiar voice from among the pile asking, "Ah, where am I? What's all these on top of me?"

"I-J? I-J?" Ida immediately reacted by rushing over to the pile to search for I-J. She almost could not find him as the bookworm had now shrunk from human-sized to the size of a normal worm, even though he was still much larger than a regular one. "What happened to you? Why are you here?"

"I jumped in after you two and bit onto your clothes as I continued to shrink. Mayhap this is the size of worms in your world," I-J remarked, sounding rather upset.

"Why? Why would you do that?" Ida asked. She did not know whether to feel consoled to have I-J around or to be concerned that I-J would probably start lecturing her about stealing a page from her own book.

"I think it's my duty to retrieve the missing page from your book..."

Oh no! Here comes the lecture.

"I take full responsibility for not taking good care of the books under my charge. I'm sorry Ms Librarian," was all I-J uttered.

Ida looked on with her jaw lightly hanging, rather surprised by the turn of events. "Erm... since you risked your life getting here, I think you have already done more than your share of the responsibility."

"No, it's not over yet. Until the day I get back the missing page, I will not rest my case," I-J said, indignantly.

"We can't get back the page! In fact, I intend to see it through that Prince Jesper change his fate!" Ida declared.

"What?! You can't change the fate of anyone! It will likely cost you your life!" exclaimed I-J.

"The fate of the nation is more important than myself. I can die and no one in the world will notice. It's just like that in class and it will be just like that with the world. It doesn't matter. So are you with me or not?" Ida demanded, making it almost clear with her gestures and expression that she was not going to take 'No' for an answer.

"Well...It is under my Book-Keeper Code that I have to follow whatever the librarian orders. I hate being a bookworm!" cursed I-J, although he did not really look that upset at his decision. "How do you intend to start?"

"Well I'm sure he will be working hard with a tutor in his room! He must have found the note by now and followed the instructions on it!" Ida said, sounding like an excitedly proud mother whose son had just graduated.

"How can we be sure? He could be lying in bed lazing around for all we know, knowing the kind of person he is," said I-J with distaste. It was clear that I-J had not got over his dislike for the prince.

"Hmm… you are right. We can't be sure unless we sneak into the palace to spy on him. But how?" Ida thought hard for a moment and looked around the room. Then she saw her reflection in the mirror and announced rather reluctantly, "I've got an idea…"

Ida's New Job

ho would have guessed that looking old had its use? By looking matured, Ida could easily apply to be a servant in the palace. Ida was alone in a room with the royal advisor; well, not really alone, as I-J was hiding in the folds on the shoulder of Ida's gown.

All around the walls were paintings of the lanky man with the curly moustache in various proud poses set against a variety of backgrounds.

"So Miss Ida Lehrer, what would you say is your specialty?" the royal advisor interviewed.

Now that was something Ida had not really given a thought about. She could not really say she was good at cleaning since her room was usually in a mess. She could not say she was good at cooking since her father was the one who did all the cooking.

"I err… I am good at reading books," answered Ida, almost sounding doubtful that the response would be of any help.

"Oh, so you're here for the new opening as a tutor for Prince Jesper?" the man questioned, suddenly studying Ida with interest.

"Yes!" Ida replied, trying her very best to sound and look assertive and confident like a tutor would.

With a sigh of relief the man said, "Oh good. I was worried about finding Prince Jesper a replacement since Mr Pfaff left yesterday claiming that our prince 'seemed like a man possessed'. The king decided to keep him home for the time being, worried about his safety around that 'creepy' library or that there really was something wrong with him. Now that's strange; we haven't even put out a notice yet."

"Err…" Ida swallowed hard before continuing, "I was sent by Wiston University. Apparently they noticed that Prince Jesper has been absent from school. Since the prince is our valued student, the school has sent me to provide personal tutorage until the prince is ready to go back to school."

The royal advisor raised an eyebrow and looked at Ida from the corner of his eye. "Hmm, I didn't know the university provides such a service."

"Yes, well we do, but I hope you would keep this hush, hush. This is but a special service extended to the prince on the grounds that he is, after all, the crown prince. We would not want the other nobles to find out about this, would we? Imagine what would happen then? Haha…" Ida said, hoping deep down inside her that it sounded convincing enough. I-J could not help but roll his eyes from his hiding spot on her gown.

The man laughed half-heartedly along and gave a few nods which seemed to say he understood before adding, "Then all I need now is to see some kind of identification before I show you to Prince Jesper."

"Identification?" Ida parroted with a stunned look.

"Show him your librarian badge!" I-J whispered to her from behind her ears.

"Oh yes. Right here!" Ida fumbled for it in the pockets on her robe. The librarian badge that her father passed her did indeed have the engraving of the university on it. Strangely, in such a brightly lit room, the magical badge did not give off any light of its own. She quickly showed the badge to the man.

"I see, a faculty council member. You look pretty young to be conferred such an honour," declared the royal advisor, who sounded rather impressed.

"Yes, my father is a professor of the school too and he started me young. Shall we begin?" Ida explained, trying to get out of this awkward situation as quickly as possible.

"Why, of course. I am delighted by your enthusiasm. This way," and the man led her out of his office. She followed him along the corridor, up a flight of stairs then passed a few rooms to a well-decorated door guarded by a pair of guards.

They immediately came to attention but the royal advisor absently waved at them and they went back to their vigilant stance.

The royal advisor knocked lightly on the door and called out, "Your Royal Highness, I've brought you your new tutor, Miss Lehrer!" Almost immediately, the door swung open and Prince Jesper's face came to view, smiling.

He looked Ida from head to toes. For a moment, she was worried that he might recognise her, but that worry instantly dissipated when he pulled her through the door then shut it behind him with a "Thanks, Kaman."

She glanced around the room which was strewn with books. Either a tornado had come through the room or Prince Jesper had really been studying.

He brought her to his desk and picked up the open book atop the pile, "Just the right person. I was figuring out what all these mean."

Ida took over the book and started concentrating on it. Prince Jesper took a closer look at her and said, "Say, have I seen you somewhere before?"

Ida jolted and quickly looked away from Prince Jesper before saying, "I believe you might have. After all, I teach at the Wiston University."

Prince Jesper continued to think hard and seemed to be digging deep into his memory well. After frowns, pouts and blinks, he seemed unable to put a finger on it as if he had totally forgotten about his classmate, Ida.

Inside her heart, Ida felt slightly hurt but she braved it on by turning back to look crossly at him and added, "Stop daydreaming and focus here."

For the rest of the day, they studied everything that interested the prince. Ida shared with him some of the topics that interested her and the prince also became fascinated with the things she taught.

At one point, Prince Jesper commented, "I never knew learning could be so entertaining."

"Then what did you like to do last time?" Ida inquired.

Prince Jesper replied, "Well I like to wrestle, or race on horses, but it's no longer fun. I guess realising that my servants were just purposely losing to me all these while took all the fun from winning." To that, both of them chuckled lightly. They were having such a good time that they did not notice that it was time for dinner until a servant knocked on the door to remind them about it!

Ida suddenly realised the time and said, "I must be off then. My father will be so worried about me."

Just as Ida was about to run off, the prince caught her arm and asked, "So nine, tomorrow morning?"

Ida beamed with pride and answered, "Yes."

The prince gave instructions to Martin to arrange for a carriage ride home. She was led down to the front door and then the gates. She realised that the forest surrounding the castle was in pitch-darkness.

In her heart, she was thankful and felt a sense of security that a tall and sturdy man who seemed to be able to carry his own weight was to be her carriage driver.

The man, smitten by Ida when he saw her, professed, "What an honour to be able to send such a beautiful lady home."

Ida was rather flattered since she had never experienced a man's attention before. She had always been 'Invisible Ida at the back of the class' so this was a first.

She looked at herself in the glass window as she was helped up the carriage. Even though she was probably in her early thirties now, she was rather attractive. *Perhaps this is what they mean by 'the charms of an older woman'.*

Then she sighed, as she sat down on the seat in the carriage and heard the door shut beside her. She had done it: she admitted that she was old and she actually liked it for a moment.

"Where to?" the carriage driver asked her after he got to the front.

"To the Wiston University quarters please," she said and then she sighed again. She was going back to the university, but she wished it was as a student in her teens.

A Trip to Town

"Ahhhhhhh!"

The scream startled I-J who was happily sleeping in a small sack made to look like a miniature bed. He fumbled for his glasses with his tail, put them on and looked around to see Ida looking at the mirror.

"What's wrong?"

"I've grown older!" was Ida's reply.

"Well I'm sure everyone grows a day older by the day," I-J said, sarcastically.

"No, look carefully!" Ida said, as she moved over to where I-J was. I-J studied her face carefully and then saw it! Some wrinkles had started to appear, though most people would probably miss them if they did not look closer. The look on I-J's face told Ida that he had seen them too.

"What happened? Did I change someone's fate when I'm not supposed to?" Ida questioned out loud.

"It appears you must have done so yesterday when you went to teach Prince Jesper! Perhaps it was fated that because of his past records of being a bad student, most tutors would have shunned him, hence by coming forth as his tutor you have altered his fate!" said I-J, thinking aloud.

"So should I still go to teach him today?" Ida said, with tears welling up in her eyes.

I-J relaxed his grimace to look up and asked, "Why not? I doubt he will notice these minor wrinkles."

"No, I mean will the curse continue to add ten years to my age if I go again today?"

"You really need to read your librarian handbook. It is clearly stated that you won't be penalised for the same offence performed on the same person. In any case, I thought you were intent on following this through?"

Ida gave a sigh of relief and resignation; I-J was right. While she had said earlier that she would be willing to give up her life to change the fate of the nation, seeing herself age so fast still scared her.

Without another word, Ida went to check on her father. It seemed that her father was feeling better but was still too frail to go back to work. In fact after that fateful night, he had become bedridden.

Ida quietly packed her bag, left her father alone to rest and headed to town for breakfast. The moment she entered town, the delicious aroma of freshly baked bread greeted her.

The town was bustling with activities with town folks going about their daily marketing as soldiers patrolled the streets and children played around the fountain.

Judging from all the splendours of the drapes and streamers used to decorate the town, the town folks were likely preparing for some big event.

Ida interrupted one of the workers to ask, "Sorry, may I ask what all these decorations are for?"

The worker laid down his bales of cloth and gaily said, "Oh haven't you heard? It's the prince's twenty-first birthday on the thirtieth of this month!"

That's interesting: Prince Jesper has the same birthday as I do!

The man continued, "He will be passing by the town in a parade and he's obliged to invite some of the girls from our town that catch his fancy to his royal birthday ball. From amongst them and the noble girls that are invited, he is to choose a wife. I believe my daughter definitely stands a chance, don't you think?" He gestured at a girl who was tying up some ribbons around the lamppost.

This caught the attention of the girl who turned around and shouted, "You dirty old man! Stop talking to some random woman and start working or I'll tell Mother you've been fooling around again!"

To that, the old man gave an apologetic nod to Ida and hurriedly continued with his chores. I-J peeped out from his usual hiding place and remarked, "If that was to be the queen one day, I think we'd all have to live as slaves."

Ida chuckled in agreement. Just then, a delicious scent of fresh bread found its way into her nose again which caused a slightly audible growl from her stomach. Instinctively, she followed the smell into a bakery.

With her first two fingers up, she ordered two loaves of breads and paid a gold coin to the baker for them. Not prepared for the gold coin, he went to the next room to get some change.

"Do you eat bread?" she asked in a whisper to I-J who was still hiding among the folds of the hood on her gown.

"What kind of a question is that? 'Do you eat bread?' Of course I don't. I'm a bookworm. Normal bookworms feed on the pages of books but we, being bookworms of the Library of Mystory are not allowed to feed on the pages of the magical books there when they are attached to the books. We're only allowed to eat them when the paper shreds come off during the magical transformation as they turn into stones," elaborated I-J, sounding rather proud of the fact that he eats paper.

Ida gave a 'what-is-there-to-be-proud-of-to-be-eating-paper' look, broke a piece of the bread and stuffed it into the hood discreetly anyway.

"Now, that is an insult to us bookworms. We..." I-J's self-righteous speech was disrupted by the fragrance of the bread. Without a second thought, he began gobbling the piece of bread.

Just then, a realisation came to Ida which made her ask, "Wait a minute, were you the reason why there seem to be holes appearing on some of my books?"

"Oh m-yes, they m-looked so deli-m-cious, I could-m-n't resist," I-J admitted, in between bites.

This caused Ida's eyes to go wide open and she would have lectured I-J if the baker had not returned with the change. "Here's your change, Miss. Is there something else that I can help you with?"

Ida took the change and replied, "Yes. Could you direct me to where I can find help to take care of my father?"

"Oh, *take care* of your father?" The baker quietly leaned forward. "Well you'll find a few such agencies down the street but I strongly recommend Assassin's Creek to *take care* of him," grinned the baker with a sinister look.

Realising what he meant by 'take care', Ida quickly clarified, "No, no, I mean to really look after him."

"Oh!" muttered the baker who suddenly looked rather disappointed. "Then perhaps try Regal Services. I heard they are the best for such boring services."

Ida nodded and thanked the man quickly before heading out of the bakery. Once she was out walking along the street, she turned her attention to I-J again, "Now, no more feeding on my books. I've bought you enough bread to last a week, considering your size."

A noise that came from among the folds of her gown suggested I-J was in agreement.

As she passed by the shops one by one, a familiar face caught her attention: Kegan was just exiting one of the agencies which seemed to provide some 'special services' as it had the signboard 'Knife's Edge: Leave the Dangerous Stuffs to Us' over its entrance.

He was followed by his servant and once out of the shop, they immediately darted into the alley beside it.

"Do you know that guy? He looked familiar," I-J asked while remaining concealed.

"That's the person who's fated to kill Prince Jesper!" responded Ida, her voice filled with anxiety.

"No wonder he looked so familiar! He doesn't seem to be up to any good."

Following I-J's words, Ida had another look at the building that Kegan exited from. It was a dilapidated building with hardly any windows. The only two windows that it had were clumsily boarded up, leaving small gaps that perhaps were meant for minimal light to get in.

"That's for sure," Ida agreed. They discreetly followed Kegan into the alley but found that he had disappeared.

"That's strange," Ida mumbled to herself. She examined all the possible hiding places but he was nowhere to be found and so had to give up searching due to time constraints. "We better find our agency soon, Prince Jesper must doubt that I'd be going by now."

It was not too difficult to find the recommended agency as it was the only one in the area that looked decently maintained. Once inside, Ida quickly approached the lady at the counter.

"Hi, I'm Corrina, what can Regal Services do for you today?" Corrina greeted as she stood up from her seat, with an awkward smile.

"My father's not feeling well today but I have to go somewhere so I need someone to take care of him."

"Oh, that's something I can help with. I used to be a lady-in-waiting for Baroness Midred," Corrina managed to speak with that plastered smile still on her face but quickly changed to a scornful face at the mention of that name and continued not-quite-under-her-breathly, "until that damn woman thought I was no better than a barmaid. Well I'll show her, I'll show her..." then as if that brief mumbling had not occurred, she looked right back up at Ida with the same smile as before.

Ida gave a look of confusion but lacked the time to bother so she asked, "Alright, so what would that cost?"

"That would be a silver piece a day, excluding expenses for food," Corrina stated, again with that smile.

Ida thought it was expensive, but her father was paid pretty well by a university for nobles so she did not feel the need to bargain. She promptly took out her coin purse and counted out the equivalent of a week worth of fees plus extra for food and said, "Here's for a week, here's the extra key to the dormitory and I'll write you the instructions and address to my place."

"Sure! Let me get a pen and some ink for you," Corrina offered, beaming with delight.

"No need for that," Ida said, remembering her self-inking pen and reached into her pocket to take it out. She took a piece of paper from the counter and began to write the relevant information before handing it over to Corrina.

Upon receiving the paper, she studied it for a while and felt the ink with curiosity, but did not dare ask too much, perhaps by virtue of her training as a lady-in-waiting. Instead she asked, "When would you like me to start?"

"Today would be great."

"Sure, I'll get right to it."

"Thank you," Ida said with a bow then made her way out of the door.

With one thing off her mind, now she could focus on the other one that was taking a toll on her life, literally.

She headed for the castle.

The Stroke

Prince Jesper was over the moon when he saw Ida. She was slightly late so he had thought that she was not coming.

As Ida came in, he put away the book, 'True Marvelland Ghost Stories' that he was reading. Ida gave a disapproving look as she hardly considered that to be worth anybody's read, but did not make her opinions known. Instead, she motioned for him to tidy up the room.

As they readied the room for lesson, Ida stole a glance at Prince Jesper. As wilful and playful as Prince Jesper was, Ida could sense that he had matured much from the time at the library. Now he was actually interested to learn from her and was absorbing everything like a sponge.

Once the room was neat, the two of them sat down and began their lesson. Hours went by, then days. Each was filled with History, Geography, Mathematics, Science and Language studies.

Ida did not know it then, but there would come a day that was to be the last of their study sessions together, and it was on that day that the prince brought up something that reminded her of what she was here for.

"Miss Lehrer, in this history book," the prince pointed out as he moved the book to share it with her, "it says that my father had actually conquered the land that belonged to the Junker family, yet gave it back. Why would he do such a silly thing?"

"Prince Jesper, this was a wise move on your father's part. He conquered the land but took away the military rights of their family. He then returned the land for them to control and prosper from it while promising military support. In return he asks for a small tribute monthly for the title of Duke. Duke Moldin Junker benefits from not having to upkeep the army, while your father benefits from his loyalty and well governance of the land, which would otherwise had been too vast for him to handle."

"But it's as if no one wins! In games, doesn't someone have to lose for another to win?" asked the prince, clearly puzzled by the concept of win-win that Ida had just explained.

She was rather shocked by the prince's perception of victory which was likely shaped by the overwhelming number of games he grew up playing. Setting a tone of seriousness, Ida sat the prince down, looked him in his eyes and said, "Prince Jesper, remember these words that I'm about to tell you. You don't always have to win to win. Sometimes, you lose more by winning."

Prince Jesper gave the look of a lost puppy, which said it all. Ida could not help but laugh.

"What's so funny?" the prince quickly asked, sounding slightly upset.

"Nothing, I'm just surprised that a person who's about to choose his wife and get married could be so naïve, that's all," said Ida, who was taking a verbal jab at the prince.

"Oh that," the prince expressed with a sigh as he leaned back on his chair, "I'm not even sure I want that – I mean how will I know who to choose? Why must they have such a stupid tradition for a prince?"

The exchange reminded Ida of the prince's final turning point and she decided to seize the moment to talk about it. "Prince Jesper, when the time comes for you to choose a wife, choose one not just for her beauty outside, but also for her beauty inside. Remember this saying that I'm about to tell you: a beautiful face may fade one day but a heart of gold will never decay."

The prince gave an even more puzzled look this time but before he could say anything, anxious knocks on the door could be heard. Before Prince Jesper could respond, the royal advisor had rushed in to announce, "Your Royal Highness, the king is in a critical condition. Come quickly!"

"Oh Kaman, don't be absurd. I just saw Father last night for dinner. How can he be in any critical condition? Can't you see that I'm busy here?" Prince Jesper asserted as he looked back at his book. Kaman was speechless.

Suddenly, Ida felt a sharp pain on her neck which could only have been caused by a bite from I-J and heard him whisper, "It's the second turning point!"

To that, Ida's eyes widened and immediately jolted into action. She went up to Kaman and quietly requested that he gave the prince some time to get changed and that he would be up in a minute. With that, Kaman bowed and exited the room with an expression that meant he highly doubted that the prince would really go.

Then she turned back to Prince Jesper with a glare and admonished him, "Look here Prince Jesper. I don't care that you are the prince or not, but this is about your father who has suddenly taken ill. By not showing concern about your father, you are being unfilial! As an unfilial prince who will be a future king, how are you going to command the respect of your subjects? Now get changed this instance and go show everyone that you care!"

"But I don't really care! We don't even talk at the dining table! How am I supposed to care?" the prince protested.

Ida bit her lips, frowned and shook her head slightly. *He has major issues!*

"Prince Jesper, would it upset you if I were to suddenly age and be gone forever?" Ida asked, staring straight into his eyes.

Prince Jesper met her gaze and thought hard about the question. "Yes, I suppose so. You've taught me so many things, I actually see you more than my parents!"

"Then if you knew I was dying, what would you do?"

"I'd quickly rush over to see you!"

"Then would you cry if you were to see me suffering and lying in bed?"

Prince Jesper quietly nodded.

"Then apply the same feeling towards your father. Your father may not have time to spend with you during the day because he is busy with court business but I understand he spends all dinners with you. Am I right?" Ida said, with added emotions.

Again the prince nodded. With a "thud" he closed his book and went on to change his clothes. Ida was shocked to see the prince strip to his undergarment and shyly turned around. "Dear Prince, you could at least have the decency to wait for me to leave the room first!"

"Oops, sorry!" snickered the prince. "My servants always help me change so I instinctively forgot that I should get you to leave first."

Once the prince was done changing, they headed hastily to the king's royal chambers. The doors were wide open and many officials were there. When one of the guards at the door saw Prince Jesper, he promptly announced the prince's arrival. This caused many of the officials to bow and move aside to allow the prince to make his way to the king's bed.

The room was filled with the smell of boiled herbs and as the prince walked towards the bed, the only sounds that could be heard were the sobbing of some of the subjects and the thumping of the prince's footsteps.

As the prince got closer, his vision began to be blurred by the accretion of his tears. When he saw how much pain his father seemed to be in, the tears overflowed and rolled down his cheeks as his knees gave way. The prince clung on to the blanket covering the king and cried, "Father! What happened? Father..."

All around him, the officials tried to console the poor boy. Kaman, looking rather surprised, began to explain, "Your Royal Highness, this morning, news of an uprising arrived at the court and it was rumoured that it was started by none other than the Junker family, a noble family with close ties to yours."

When the prince heard the family name, he looked up and asked, "Junker? Do they have a son by the name of Kegan?"

"Yes, Your Royal Highness, I believe you might have met him as he's about your age and studies at the university you attend," one of the officials confirmed with a look of cognizance. He was likely in charge of education.

"Though it was only a rumour, it was nonetheless too much to bear to be betrayed by a close friend that Your Majesty had a stroke right on the spot," added another official who had a face with sorrow written all over it.

"What have we done about the uprising?" asked the sincerely worried Prince Jesper. The question raised a few eyebrows as the officials hardly expected the prince to take an interest in state matters. They turned to look at a man in a well-decorated soldier uniform who was likely the general.

The question seemed to have caught him by surprise as he cleared his throat before saying, "Well, Your Royal Highness, the uprising has been squelched and no evidence has been found to confirm that it was instigated by the Junkers but we have brought in a few men for questioning."

"That's good to hear. Bring me to see these men," Prince Jesper commanded. It was clear that the men in the room were filled with awe and respect for the suddenly matured prince as the general led him out of the room and many of the officials followed.

Ida took a look at the king's face. The weariness on his face reminded her of her own father who was sick back home. From inside her gown, I-J sneaked out to have a peek. He whispered, "He seems to be in a better condition than what we saw in the pictures."

This made Ida realise something, so she quietly sneaked out of the room and made her way back home.

The Showdown

he next morning, there was no scream. She had, after all, realised that this was what would happen when she directed the prince to head over to the royal chambers.

By now, strands of white hair had developed all over her head. The wrinkles on her face had become even more prominent. While there did not seem to be a huge difference between her last two transformation, there really was a stark difference between how she looked today and yesterday.

She just sat there looking at herself in the mirror and cried softly. It was only much later that I-J woke up with a sleepy stretch and yawned. "Ah, it feels so good to finally be able to sleep-in late without having to worry about putting books back at the right place."

He then looked around and realised that Ida was sitting silently before the mirror. He wriggled up beside her to find tears dripping from her jaw.

"Ida? Are you ok?" I-J asked. When Ida did not reply, he turned to examine Ida's reflection in the mirror.

Then a wave of shock hit him and he gasped, "You've aged again!"

"Yes," Ida replied, with a tone of resignation. There was a long silence as each of them had a knowing look on their face as to why this would have happened: Ida had changed the fate of Prince Jesper when she intervened and demanded him to go visit his sick father.

Then after quite a while, Ida said, "I don't think I can go tutor him today. Prince Jesper will definitely get a fright if he realised I've grown ten years in a day."

I-J replied with a silent nod.

Just then, the rustling sound of metal keys could be heard as the door knob began to turn. Ida panicked as she was not used to having visitors since she stayed alone with her father. She stood up while turning to see who it was. Beside her, I-J hastily hid behind a box on the dressing table.

Ida came face-to-face with a startled look on a familiar face. The person quickly composed herself and greeted, "Greetings. I'm Corinna from Regal Services. You must be Mrs Lehrer. Your daughter arranged for me to come take care of your husband and I've been diligently doing so for the past few days while you were away."

Ida's mouth twitched to the fact that the lady could not recognise her anymore and now she was old enough to be recognised as her own father's wife. However, she knew there was no one else she could pretend to be and hence, hesitantly nodded in acknowledgement.

Corinna closed the door behind her and placed her bagful of food on the table to unpack it. She seemed to be in a gleeful mood as she hummed while going about her task.

"Sure is an eventful day for me," Corinna suddenly mentioned, "meeting the mistress of the house for the first time." She took a quick glance at Ida and smiled before looking back down and continuing with what she was doing.

"Not to mention, people were snagging up the foodstuffs in the market because of the recent rebellion. Almost every stall was sold out today so I had to pay nearly double to get these vegetables," Corinna revealed as she raised the vegetables to show Ida. She seemed to be hinting that Ida should be paying her extra for the day.

Taking the hint, Ida searched for her purse and took out some money quickly to pay Corinna.

After checking that she had received the right amount, Corinna looked at Ida again, smiled the same meaningful smile before putting the money into her pockets. Then she added with excitement, "To top it all up, I saw the crown prince quarrelling on the streets with a noble. How often do we commoners ever get to see royalties behave like that?"

"Wait a minute, are you talking about Prince Jesper? Who was he quarrelling with on the streets?" Ida asked, suddenly attentive.

"Yes! I believe he was quarrelling with the noble from the Junker family about inciting the recent rebellion or something. Haha! What nonsense. Everyone knows that the Junker family and the ruling Koenig family go way back," Corinna said as she went about sorting out the foodstuffs on the table into baskets and different containers.

Ida looked down to where I-J was hiding and it was clear that the both of them were thinking the same thing: *the third turning point!* Ida secretly picked I-J up and excused herself to leave the house.

She ran towards town as fast as her old legs could take her. Some of the town folks that she passed gave a curious look, on seeing a lady of her age run like that.

By the time she reached the town gate, she was already out of breath. Thankfully, she did not have to search far to find where Prince Jesper and Kegan were having their row, for right by the large fountain, a huge crowd had gathered.

Prince Jesper and Kegan had taken off their coats and doublets and stood at different corners of the fountain basin which was filled with water to shin-level.

Before long, Martin stood out to address the crowd and the two competitors, "The prince has agreed to a friendly wrestle with Lord Kegan Junker and the boundary, as agreed upon by them, will be the circumference of this fountain. The last man standing in the fountain will be the winner."

"And the loser," Prince Jesper added spitefully with his index finger pointing at Kegan, "will have to admit to his crimes."

"Ha! Ha! And should you lose, you will have to apologise to me in front of everyone here and clear my name," retorted Kegan.

"Enough with the talking, let's see what you're really made of," challenged the prince. To that, both of them walked towards the middle of the fountain where a beautiful statue of an angel, pouring a never-ending supply of water from her pot at waist-level, separated the two.

With a whistle, Martin commenced the duel. The two danced cautious steps around the statue, growling as they faked their advances. Then Kegan, with a well-timed splash of the water, temporarily blinded Prince Jesper and took the opportunity to lunge forward.

Though blinded, Prince Jesper was fully aware of Kegan's every move by listening to the splatter of water that followed Kegan's every move. He dodged Kegan's next attack by rolling sideways and blinked his eyes into clarity. The missed punch caused Kegan to temporarily lose his footing and gave Prince Jesper enough time to regain his composure. He then sprung at Kegan by using his shoulders to push him towards the knee-high wall that marked the boundary of the fountain.

Kegan grabbed the prince's shoulders and pushed his right foot backwards to stabilise himself and soon found it against the wall. With force, he resisted the prince's advance and was able to bring it to a standstill. For a moment it seemed that no one had the upper hand.

With a boost from his back kick, Kegan managed to push the prince away from him. The prince steadied himself and immediately went at Kegan again. Kegan tried to dodge but was slightly too slow and was thrown down into the water by Prince Jesper. He looked down at Kegan without showing any sign of compassion— his fighting stance still as unwavering.

Ida had tried to squeeze her way as far into the crowd as she could but ended up being expelled to the back of the crowd again. It did not help that her body was not as strong as it used to be.

Eventually she gave up and just stood where she was to listen to the grunts of both men and the splashing of water to paint a mental picture of the fight that was going on.

From the cheers of "Way to go Prince Jesper!" from the crowd, Ida knew that Prince Jesper was now having the upper hand and she could tell what was about to happen – the prince was going to win and if he wins, Kegan was not going to be pleased with that.

In that instance, she made up her mind. With a deep breath, Ida summoned all her latent strength and yelled, "Prince Jesper, you don't always have to win to win!"

At that, everyone turned around to find the owner of that voice. Ida imitated their actions and turned around too. When the crowd could not seem to identify the source of the shout, they lost interest and turned their attention back to the fight.

Prince Jesper looked up as his frown softened to a look of query. While he was focused on winning his opponent just a moment ago, his mind was now filled with questions about the owner of the voice that sounded suspiciously like Miss Lehrer.

You don't always have to win to win. Sometimes, you lose more by winning.

He had not seen Miss Lehrer since yesterday. She did not come by nine this morning so he had sent his men to make an enquiry at Wiston University, but the staff there told them that there was no such person. The only person that was a Lehrer was Professor Lehrer, his former teacher.

When his men came back with that information, he came to town to personally search for Miss Lehrer with his men. That was when he met Kegan and had a heated argument with him which resulted in this wrestling challenge.

Somehow there seemed to be someone he was forgetting. A faint image of a young red-headed girl whose name he scarcely remembered appeared in this mind.

Then the sound of someone trying to get himself back on his feet in a pool of water interrupted Prince Jesper's thoughts.

His opponent was up, but it was clear he was in no condition to win anymore. Yet with his heavy breath and scowling face, it was also clear that losing was not an option to him. With a loud roar, he made a charge at Prince Jesper.

Prince Jesper readied his stance but it was a different stance this time – he was going to tackle Kegan head-on instead. In a flash, Prince Jesper ran at Kegan and pushed him back to the edge of the fountain. Then the prince made a doubtful misstep, which sent the both of them tumbling to the dry ground beyond the boundary of the fountain.

Martin was speechless, as was the crowd. Prince Jesper stood up, dusted himself on the shoulders and declared, "It seems I've met my worthy competitor today. There will be no losers today."

He then took two steps towards Kegan, who was struggling to get up, and extended his right hand. Kegan's gaze followed the shoes up the length of the prince's legs to his outstretched hands. Kegan looked back down on the floor as he took the assistance from the prince to get up.

Once he got up, the prince continued his grasp on Kegan's hands and raised it above both their heads. The crowd was slow to begin cheering but eventually it caught on as they cheered loudly in unison. A faint smile broke out on Kegan's face. He gave a slow, quiet nod to the prince, who smiled back and returned the nod.

The Parade

da did not even bother to look in the mirror for she knew what she would see and ageing ten years overnight was not a pretty sight.

If she were to make a guess, she was probably sixty-one as she could feel her body reacting much slower than she was used to and the back of her hand was starting to look like dried prunes.

She had gotten up early to prepare to leave for town in order to avoid bumping into Corrina. That day happened to be the day of the prince's parade and the day after was to be his birthday ball. Coincidentally, her birthday was on the same day as Prince Jesper's which meant she was exactly one year older than him.

Two more turning points, she thought as she packed her bag. She was beginning to wonder if she could live to see everything through and even celebrate her birthday after the ball. Sadly, she knew that no one will probably know about the sacrifice that she had made, but she guessed she did not mind since alternatively she would just be 'Invisible Ida who sat at the back of the class' and both roles were equally insignificant.

At least now she felt like a heroine. *A lonely dying heroine whose heroic deeds no one even knew about.* She gave an ironic laughter at that thought.

She finished packing, gave a kiss on her sleeping father's forehead and left her dormitory with I-J.

As she was staggering down the hill on which the university sat atop, I-J saw Corrina walking up the path that followed the slope. "Look Ida, it's Corrina!"

Ida quickly hid her face further into her hood and hoped Corrina would not identify her and thankfully she did not as she passed Ida and continued her journey up the slope with her basket of groceries, occasionally cursing the slope for being steep.

The walk to town took much longer than usual, understandably so given her condition now. By the time she reached the gate, the guards have already secured the area, clearing the middle of the road to await the prince's arrival. Town folks watching the parade had form on either side of the road, behind two lines of guards.

Ida was directed to form up with the town folks, but she found herself hunched and not being able to see much from behind the crowd.

"Every one of those girls seems to be dressed to the teeth," I-J remarked as he peeped out from Ida's hood to have a look.

This brought Ida's attention to the many young girls who were inching their way to the front of the crowd but behind the line of guards. Many were dressed to impress and they definitely spared no expense in doing so; with sequin dresses, big feathery hats and thick makeup, one might have mistaken them for nobles, though it must have burned a big hole in their parents' pockets.

Ida wondered if she would have done the same if she were twenty-one still. Then again, she would probably be holed up in the library that very instance.

Then she thought of the Library of Mystory. *Sigh, why did I have to enter that cursed place?*

Sudden loud cheers brought Ida back to reality. She tiptoed to try to see what had caused the cheers but to no avail. She could feel I-J crawling up her hair to the top of her head under the hood to try to catch a glimpse of what had happened. Right behind them, a man gave a weird look when he observed a bulge under Ida's hood, wriggling about.

"Do you see anything?" Ida whispered to I-J as she rolled her eyes upwards in an effort to see him.

"Yes. I see a figure of a man on a horse flanked by two other horse riders," I-J responded, as quietly as he could yet audible to Ida amidst the noise.

The girls' screams of "It's the prince!" began to die down as the figure drew near and talks of "Oh, it's just the royal advisor" replaced the screams.

Soon the royal advisor stopped his horse in the middle of the road as his guards followed suit. Then he cleared his throat and announced, "Dear citizens of Marvelland, the prince will be arriving soon. As he goes on his parade, he will choose five lucky girls from among you who will be invited to attend his ball. Should he point to you, kindly step out in front of the guards and someone will escort you to a carriage."

From the daze that some of the girls seemed to be in, it was obvious that they were already counting their chickens before they were hatched.

However, Ida was not focused on these girls – she was looking out for the old lady that the prince was supposed to be saving today. Interestingly, despite the overwhelming crowd, there were hardly any old folks, much less any old lady. Most of the older folks must have chosen to avoid the parade as they probably knew that it would be too crowded for their brittle bones.

The sky was starting to get dark with the clouds ready to let go of all the condensate they had been storing up at any moment, but neither the prince nor the old lady was in sight.

Ida realised she need a better vantage point. Looking around, she saw some crates stacked neatly beside a watermill that could aid her in climbing to the roof of the watermill.

She broke away from the crowd and started climbing the crates. As she was reaching out for a tile on the roof, her right hand slipped but she instantly made a grab for a brick that was slightly jutting out, saving her from tumbling down the crates.

"Mind you! Be careful! You're no longer any younger you know!" reminded I-J harshly.

Ida sucked in a breath of air through her teeth and rolled her eyes. "Thanks for stating the obvious."

She continued her climb and reached the roof. She crawled up unsteadily, made worse by the strong wind that was now howling through the whole town.

"What's happening?" I-J asked, evidently bothered by the wind that was causing the hood to constantly slap his face.

However it took a short while before Ida understood what he was asking to reply, "It's about to rain."

"What's rain?" I-J continued to ask. It was clear he had never experienced such a thing before in the library. Right at the moment when he asked, little droplets of water began to fall from the sky.

"*This* is rain," Ida answered, motioning to what was happening around her.

Then the little droplets became larger until it became a downpour. Beside them, the river began to furiously batter the mill, turning the wheel like those of a moving carriage.

Ida scanned the area worriedly. The rain reduced her visibility considerably and from this far away, she could not see much of the parade, though she did have a good view of the gate.

Then, she saw him and the screams of the girls affirmed that: the prince was here.

Now the problem was, where's the old lady? She stood up on the roof to get a better view but there definitely was no old lady in the crowd or anywhere nearby.

"Do you see any old lady?" Ida asked.

"No!" I-J answered, still struggling with the effects of the wind and rain.

The prince was already halfway through the parade and the absence of the old lady was getting more nerve-wracking by the minute.

She closed her eyes and covered her face with her hands, thinking hard. *Where is this old lady who's supposed to be drowning in the river?* Her hands absently caressed the wrinkles on her face as she went through her thought. Then suddenly, she opened her eyes wide with a look of horror and realisation.

The sudden realisation hit her like a ton of brick, causing her to stagger backwards involuntarily. With a sudden gust of wind combined with the sudden clash of a wave of the river on the watermill, she dove into the river, missing the wheel by a hair.

I-J reacted just in time by jumping out of her hood and landing safely onto the roof. When he turned back, Ida was nowhere to be seen among the torrential waves of the gushing river.

Rescuing the Old Lady

rince Jesper had scorned at the idea of the parade. It was after much persuasion from his father, who had been recovering well, that he finally agreed to do it, hence the delay.

By now, the storm had gotten quite powerful. The prince took a deep breath before giving a sigh. *A prince's gotta do what a prince's gotta do.*

He entered the gate to the screams of hundreds of female admirers, reaching their hands out from behind the line of guards to try to touch the prince or get his attention. The rain had smudged most of their makeup and the sight was like a scene from the book 'True Marvelland Ghost Stories' he had read recently.

He shuddered as he tried to avoid their hands from left and right and elongated his lips in a half-hearted effort to put on a smile.

Further along the path was Kaman, who rode his horse back to meet the prince. After seeing the prince's reaction to the parade, he turned his horse around to align it side-by-side with the prince's horse.

He leaned in and whispered to the prince, "Smile dignifiedly and remember you've got to pick out five girls to bring to the ball!"

The prince said with his mouth agape, "What? How? Who am I going to pick among *these*?" His eyes guided Kaman's to the lines of girls and it was evident in the royal advisor's facial expression that it was really not as straightforward as he had expected.

After much consideration, Kaman leaned in again and whispered to the prince, "It's only customary; most crown princes

wouldn't marry commoners. Just choose anyone with a good figure."
Then he quickened the pace of his horse to go ahead. It almost
seemed like he did not want to answer any more questions from the
prince.

The prince watched as Kaman repeated to the town folks
in front of him, "The prince will be passing by shortly, please be
patient." Then he turned his focus back to the task at hand and
began to point out the first girl. Her reaction was one of elation and
she screamed as she came forward to the front of the line to be led
away by a guard.

This brought louder screams from the line across the path
and so the prince brought his attention over to the other side and
randomly chose a girl.

This was easier than he thought! Three more and he could
finally go home!

I-J could not see a thing through the darkness. The howling
wind and crushing waves made it almost impossible to hear
anything else.

Ida was down in the water somewhere and hopefully she was
still clinging on to something for her dear life. I-J had no time to
lose and, near immediately, made up his mind to get to the prince.

He looked around and tried to devise a plan. The buildings
were arranged in neat rows, parallel to each other. The watermill
was the first in a row of buildings nearest to the river. The prince
was going along the pathway beside the second row of buildings.
However, they all converged at the town centre, marked by the
fountain that Prince Jesper and Kegan dueled at and Prince Jesper
was about to pass the fountain. If only I-J could get to the end of his
row of buildings that very moment, he might still be able to reach
the prince.

I-J looked harder and found that rain-gutters ran along the roof of all the buildings. He turned around and found a big fallen leaf. Now all he had to do was to find his courage.

Now is not the time to be afraid. Miss Librarian needs me!

He took a deep breath and jumped into the rain gutter with the fallen leaf under him. He allowed the flowing rainwater to carry him along the rain gutter. Right before the rainwater entered a pipe, he made a jump with the leaf to reach the rain gutter of the next roof. He did this over and over again until it got him to the house right behind the line of the crowd. Then once the rainwater was about to enter the drainage pipe, he jumped for the hand of one of the girls in the crowd.

He landed on her arm instead. That instant, when the lady felt something land on her arm, she instinctively turned her attention to it to find out what it was. Her scream immediately changed from one that was begging for the attention of the prince, to one of fright. She immediately flung her arms to get rid of the worm.

I-J got the boost that he needed and landed on another girl's arms. The same reaction ensued and he was flung to another girl's arms. This went on for a while until he was finally flung onto something that did not fling him away!

By then, I-J was dizzy from being flung around and his head was spinning. He shook off the giddiness and realised that he was right on the prince's left shoulders! The prince was pointing to a girl from among the crowd with his right index finger. That was the fourth girl he had chosen thus far.

He wriggled up near the prince's ears and spoke in a hollow voice, "Dear prince, please help! There's a woman who had fallen into the river!"

⊰✦⊱

The prince jerked back and twisted his head and body around to look behind for the owner of the voice. He gave an inquisitive look to the guard on his left who returned an equally curious look at the prince.

Then the voice came again. "Stop looking for me. You won't find me anywhere. I am the voice of the..." I-J hesitated for a moment to think but decided that nothing scared him more than... "*Ghostly Rain*. I'm telling you there's no time to lose! Quick! Save the woman before she drowns in the river."

After seeing the horde of defaced succubus screaming at him and having read the 'True Marvelland Ghost Stories' recently, Prince Jesper was ready to believe anything. He glanced around to find the river and called out, "Guards, to the river! A woman is drowning!"

With a light kick to the horse's side, the prince galloped off with his two guards following suit, leaving the rows of girls wondering what had happened.

They followed the path to the edge of the town and turned left to where the river was and travelled along its bank.

"She fell in from the watermill," said the voice.

Prince Jesper called out to one of his guards and directed him towards the mill. The storm had eased up but the river current was still too strong to catch sight of anything.

"Let's follow the river downstream! Keep your eyes peeled for a woman!" commanded the prince.

This led them back into the town but down another lane which ran parallel to the river banks. The lane was laid behind the rows of buildings of which their rain gutters I-J had used to surf into town.

The prince galloped back and forth along the path looking for any signs of a woman. "Any signs?" he asked one of his men, who shook his head in reply and they went on with their search.

Soon the prince feared the worst – that she may have been swept further downstream or she had gone under the currents – and, at the same time, started to wonder if he had gone mad for listening to the howls of the wind, telling him about some drowning lady.

It was then that he noticed a beam of light!

Ida had plunged into the water several times after she fell in. The current was too strong and there was nothing she could do except to try to catch her breath and stay afloat.

The current had carried her quite a distance until she was swept up against the branches of a fallen tree that was sprawled across the river. She quickly grabbed on tightly to the branches.

She tried to climb up to the trunk a few times but the branches were too slippery and her hands were not strong enough to pull herself up. As such, she continued to hold on to the branches for her dear life.

Soon, however, her hands began to tremble from exhaustion. In the distance, she could make out the silhouette of the town and there seemed to be a flurry of people looking for something in the river. *Perhaps they are searching for me!*

Ida looked everywhere for something that would catch their attention and it was then that she noticed, inside the pocket of her robe, her librarian badge gleaming away.

She clutched on to the branches with her right underarms and used her left hand to reach into her pocket to take out the badge and wave it feverishly at the silhouette of the people who seemed to be looking for her.

Then the figure, which seemed to have caught sight of her signal, travelled with great haste towards her. Soon, she was able to make out who it was.

It was Prince Jesper!

Without waiting for the others, Prince Jesper galloped his horse towards the beam of light. Behind him, he could hear his men chasing him and it seemed some of the town folks had also gotten in on the action.

He was glad when he saw that it was really an old lady clutching on the branches of a fallen tree with her right underarms and holding some light-emitting item on her left hand. He was not in the mind to bother what the item was as he took the rope from his horse saddlebag. It was a good thing he often hunted and kept ropes in his horse saddlebag to tie up his catches.

He threw one end of the rope right to the old lady, who had put away her bright object to grab hold of the rope with her left hand. He then tied the other end of the rope around a small tree.

"Tie the rope around your waist. I'll pull you in!" shouted the prince. The woman struggled to do as she was told but eventually managed to make a tight knot around herself.

Around then, the prince's men and some of the town folks arrived and they quickly came forward to help pull the woman up from the river.

When the woman was near the bank, Prince Jesper offered his right hand to her. The woman saw his hand and reached out her right hand to grab his. With a strong pull, Prince Jesper pulled the old woman up from the waters and into his arms.

This brought them face-to-face with each other and suddenly a wave of recognition swept him, but he could not be sure as this woman was at least twenty years older than Miss Lehrer!

"Miss Lehrer?" the prince said, almost as a question, as he gave an audible gasp.

The woman immediately turned away but before he could say a word or take another look, the town folks all lifted him up and hailed him as a hero. As he was being brought away to the tavern, he grabbed one of his guards by his shoulder and whispered something to his ear.

"We should go."

Ida looked down for the source of the voice and there was I-J, looking rather shaken. In the midst of it all, I-J had quietly jumped off the back of the prince and crawled up to Ida.

Ida knew he was right and picked I-J up. She gently placed him in her hood and was about to leave when a guard stopped her in her tracks.

"Madam, the prince has selected you as the fifth lady to be invited for the ball."

Ida reached into her pockets and took out her librarian badge to shine into the eyes of the guard. He was temporarily blinded as Ida ran to hide behind some barrels.

She waited till the guard had passed her hiding spot before she felt it was safe enough to come out and walked gingerly home.

Before the Ball

"Ahhhhhhh!"

The scream startled Ida who was lying in bed feeling aches and sores all over. Luckily her father slept in the other room and her door was closed.

She dragged herself up from the bed and walked to the mirror where I-J was.

"What's wrong?" Ida asked listlessly.

"What's wrong? What's WRONG?! Look at the number of wrinkles I've grown over night!" replied I-J, irate with Ida for even asking such a question with an obvious answer.

Ida looked in the mirror and studied I-J. Honestly she could not see any difference. A worm was just a worm like any other worm to her. However, taking a glance at the mirror made her see something she had sworn off doing: she sneaked a peek at herself and immediately regretted it.

She probably looked seventy-one, frail and shrivelled. Her hair was now blondish and she was slightly hunched.

Tears were now flowing freely down her cheeks so much so that I-J reactively asked, "Does rain happen indoors too?" Then he looked up to find the source of the water drops and with sudden realisation, his misery did not feel as miserable anymore.

It seemed that I-J was now able to understand Ida's plight better after being cursed for knowingly taking actions to change the prince's fate.

They both shared a moment of silent grief, exchanging thousands of unspoken regrets, worries and angry words.

Then the moment was interrupted by the rustling of keys. Ida knew who to expect this time and had already planned on what to do and say.

"Oh my," Corrina opened the door, slightly shocked to see the fairly unrecognisable figure, "is that you Mrs Lehrer?"

"Yes, Corrina, come in," Ida said as she slid over to cover I-J with her body. I-J took the hint and jumped onto her robe and crawled up.

"My! My! Look at you; you look like you've aged twenty years in a day!" Corrina said. She was not wrong to have that perception, especially since they had skipped a day of meeting each other.

"Oh, I'm planning to go to Prince Jesper's ball disguised as some old noble woman," came Ida's reply without missing a beat. "It must have been very convincing!"

"Not with that outfit. Did I ever tell you I used to be a lady-in-waiting for Baroness Midred," Corrina's signature fake smile quickly changed to that scornful face at the mention of that name and muttered, "Until that damn woman thought I was no better than a barmaid. Well I'll show her, I'll show her…"

"Yes, I believe you did," Ida infectiously copied the fake smile in reply.

"'You look more like a barmaid than anything' is what she would have said." Before Ida could react, Corrina was ransacking through her closet, digging out dresses that her mother had left behind. It was a good thing that after all these years, her father did not throw away anything that belonged to her mother even though he said she had died at child birth.

All that noise seemed to have awakened her father who was at the door to his room, leaning on the frame for support and asking, "What's going on here?"

Corrina looked up from what she was doing and said, "Oh Professor Lehrer! I'm so sorry to have stirred you from your sleep. Your wife here is planning on attending the prince's birthday ball in that drab."

"Sarah?" Ida's father looked at Ida for a moment, his eyes filled with longing, but that soon turned to realisation, then shock.

Ida quickly went over to him and brought him back into the room, then closed the door behind her. As she led him to sit on one of the two chairs by the table in the room, Ida's father's hands grabbed on tightly to hers and his eyes glued to her face.

After they sat, Ida's father began to sob and whispered, "Oh Ida, what have I done to you!"

"It's alright, Father. Tonight is the last turning point. Once I'm done, the country will be safe," Ida said, trembling as she tried her very best to remain strong before her father.

"I...but...," he was at a loss for words and began to search the floor for them.

As Ida bent to meet his father's eyes, all she could see was sorrow and guilt. She understood that he must be pained by his decision to get Ida involved. "Father, you have allowed me to lead a more meaningful life than I would have lived before. I thank you Father, from the bottom of my heart."

He looked up from the floor, his eyes now a well of tears ready to overflow at any time. "Ida, you're even older than I am now. Perhaps for this last turning point, let me take care of it, or at least let me help you. Just tell me what to do."

"Father, it's fine. I've got it all planned...," Ida's words trailed off as she considered something for a moment. "Hmm, perhaps there *is* something that you can me help with!"

Finding Madelief

arriages pulled up one after another and out from them came ladies and gentlemen all dressed to the nines. Ladies came in their silk dresses with jewellery well displayed while the gentlemen came in their stylish dress-coat and matching pants.

Ida and her father fitted right in with their dressing but stood out like a sore thumb, in terms of their age, much like their horse cart in the line of carriages.

They would have to thank Corrina who managed to get everything ready by pulling a few strings. The only blemish was of course the horse cart as Corrina had plainly put it, "Every cursed carriage has been booked up for use to go to this stupid ball."

Interestingly, the door man who welcomed them did not even bat an eyelid, perhaps well-trained enough to not offend any of the prestigious guests that may turn up.

They were assisted down from their horse cart and directed to the door. Ida stared at the guards and swallowed hard, worried that she might be barred from entering. There was one standing at attention on each side of the door but none of them made any effort to stop them from entering. Ida gave a look of relief as the two of them walked casually past the guards, but she was slightly disappointed as she had wanted to see the look of surprise on the guards' face when she told them she was the fifth lady selected by the prince.

Interestingly, every young lady that tried to gain entrance was stopped and had her name checked against a list before she was allowed entry.

Inside the ballroom, nothing short of grandeur could be seen: a spacious room was decorated with banners and drapes of the colours in season, boasting a ceiling nearly twice as high as the grand stairway at the far end of the room. In the middle of the room, framed by a large orchestra, was the dance floor where a large chandelier hung above.

Immediately, Ida's eyes scanned the ballroom, in search of any familiar faces. The guests were seemingly clustered according to age group and so Ida knew to look out for people her age – well, her original age.

"Look for Madelief," Ida whispered as she tilted her face towards her father but kept her eyes to the front.

"Madelief? Why her?" her father asked out of curiousity.

"Well, of all the girls of noble birth in the class, I liked her the most," explained Ida. "At least she wasn't snobbish."

Professor Lehrer did not want to argue with that and he began looking earnestly around the ballroom. Even I-J was peeping out from his hiding place from amongst Ida's hive of a hair, though he was more intent on looking at what was going on around him.

Then suddenly, Professor Lehrer exclaimed quietly, "There!" as he pointed at a group of young ladies. Ida's eyes followed her father to where he pointed and found Madelief.

"Stay here, Father," she said as she handed her father her coat and lumbered slowly to where the ladies were.

Once she was near enough to Madelief, she pretended to trip and fall right beside her.

"Oh dear Madame, are you alright?" Madelief hurriedly kneeled to pick Ida up.

"Oh thank you Miss. Could you help me to that chair over there?" Ida spoke in a feeble voice as she gestured to a chair at the corner of the room.

Madelief looked around for help but the other ladies were feigning ignorance.

Madelief looked back at Ida and with a smile, assisted her to the chair. Once there, Ida suddenly pulled her closer and whispered, "Madelief, it's me, Ida. I need your help."

Madelief could not conceal the look of bewilderment and doubt on her face. "Ida? Are you sure? What happened to you?"

"I don't have time to explain, but I need you to make sure the prince chooses you to marry."

"How am I supposed to do that? It's not up to me to decide who he marries," Madelief said, sounding rather unconvinced.

"When he dances with you later, mention the following sentence and he will."

"What sentence?"

"A beautiful face may fade one day but a heart of gold will never decay."

"What? Why that…" Madelief's question was interrupted by the sounding of trumpets and the royal advisor announcing the arrival of the crown prince. She, like everyone in the ballroom, turned to face the grand stairway and clapped to welcome the prince.

When she turned back, Ida was already gone.

Even though the night was still young, Prince Jesper had already danced with half a dozen ladies. Kaman had explained to him the rules of the ball - that he had to dance with every eligible lady in the room, pretend to show interest in them and make small talks, then before the end of the night, retire to his chamber, get changed and think about which lady he would take as her wife. Then when the clock strikes twelve, he will make his grand entrance once again to announce his decision. After that, he will invite the lady who would be his bride up on stage, kiss her before the crowd to seal the deal and live happily ever after with her.

Sounds simple enough? Except that it really was not. All of the ladies he had danced with were obviously reciting carefully scripted lines to impress him.

When it was time to dance with some of his classmates, Evalia, of course, demanded to go first, to which the prince willingly obliged. Of all the girls, he found Evalia to be the most attractive. Still, he was not sure how she was like as a person.

"You know, one of my favourite pastimes is horse riding," Evalia said during the dance, to which the prince reacted with surprise. *A girl that likes horse riding. Hmm, interesting.*

"Really? We should go try that now!"

"Don't worry, you'll have lots of opportunities in the future," she replied with a wink as she finished the dance and waltzed away.

Prince Jesper was still smiling to himself when Madelief came over for her dance. "Prince Jesper? Prince Jesper?" Madelief called for his attention.

Prince Jesper snapped out of his trance and found her in his arms ready to start the dance. There was some awkwardness for the first few moments and it seemed like something was bothering Madelief.

"Prince Jesper, do you remember Ida?"

"Ida who?" Somehow the name rang a bell but he just could not put a face to it.

"Never mind. She was our classmate but she and her father stopped coming to school the day after they found you in that library. Anyway I just saw her, or at least I thought I saw her."

"What's so surprising about that?"

"It was a very old lady who claimed to be Ida and she told me to tell you something such that you will choose me as your wife."

Prince Jesper gave a polite laugh and asked, "And what might that be?"

"A beautiful face may fade one day but a heart of gold will never decay."

The prince dropped Madelief's hands and stopped dancing as he stood there with his jaw stuck open.

Madelief took that as a sign that the prince wanted to stop dancing and so did a curtsey before she quickly excused herself, worried that she might have said something to offend the prince.

Meanwhile the prince could not concentrate on dancing with his next dance partner, Jalena. Even though she tried to make small talks, the prince did not respond to any.

Soon, the clock struck eleven, and the royal advisor announced that it was time for the prince to retire to his chambers and consider his options.

The prince ran back to his room clearly with a lot on his mind.

As the Clock Strikes Twelve

da saw Madelief dance with the prince and also his reaction to something she had said to him. *It must have worked.*

The moment the prince retired to his chambers, the king went up on stage, which was actually the landing of the grand stairway, to give a speech, thanking everyone for their concern over his health and for attending the crown prince's grand birthday ball.

"We should leave now," I-J whispered to Ida, who nodded in agreement. She tucked at her father's sleeves and said the same thing but his reaction was much different from hers.

"No! The king is speaking now; it would be disrespectful if we were to leave now. In any case, the guards won't be opening the door until the ball is over."

Ida turned around to look at the door and true enough, it was closed. Unfortunately, this meant that she had to spend a much longer time hiding from Madelief who was going around looking for her.

Luckily for Ida, growing old had caused her to hunch and she could easily hide behind her father, who was in disguise, to avoid a direct view from Madelief.

She just wished the ball would be over sooner.

"Prince Jesper, which suit would you like to wear?" Martin asked as he gestured to two suits held out by two other servants.

Prince Jesper was in no mood to care.

Ida. Who is this Ida? Why can't I remember her? How did she know what Miss Lehrer told me?

Then a bright green glow came from his closet, which startled everyone in the room, including the prince.

"What was that?" the prince asked.

Martin slowly inched closer to the closet then in one swift motion, opened the closet door to reveal a gown.

"That's the gown that you wore the day you passed out from the library," pointed out one of the servants.

"What is it doing here?" Prince Jesper asked.

"When we tried to change you out of your gown, you clung on to it and kept mumbling, 'Something important. Something important.' and so we didn't dare wash it," the servant explained.

Prince Jesper looked at Martin to verify the servant's words and Martin gave an affirmative nod. The prince strode forward to the closet and took out the gown to examine it.

He reached his hands into one of the pockets and took out a folded piece of paper as Martin and the servants stepped closer to have a better look.

The prince unfolded the paper and saw moving images of an old lady talking to Madelief. Then the image changed to another of the old lady hiding behind a pillar while watching the prince and Madelief dance.

Then he saw the old lady looking up at him as he said something on the grand stairway to the cheering gestures of the crowd. After that, the old lady suddenly grew even older and collapsed on the spot with a smile still on her face.

He turned the paper and on the other side were the following words:

> 1) Take your studies seriously
> 2) Show your love for your father
> 3) Make friends with Kegan
> 4) Save an old lady from drowning
> 5) Choose the right wife

Then he realised that at corner of the page was the name 'Ida Lehrer' and the number '82' while the number '81' was on the previous.

With a sudden tenacity, the prince ordered, "Quick Martin, get me dressed. I know what I must do now."

The king just would not stop talking! It was to the relief of many when the royal advisor suddenly scrambled down the grand stairway to whisper into the king's ear, to which, the king's surprised response were, "So soon? Why, alright then!"

Kaman then took the stage to announce, "Dear distinguished guests, the crown prince has decided on his bride! Please welcome again, Prince Jesper!"

Ida snuck out from her hiding place behind her father to see the prince walk down the grand stairway to the applause of the crowd.

Slowly, the applause died down as the prince reached the center of the stage.

He cleared his throat and began, "Today, I've had the honour to dance with many of you fine ladies and at the end of tonight, I am to decide on one who will be my bride. It was a difficult decision for me to make as many of you were beautiful in your own rights. Someone once told me, that 'a beautiful face may fade one day but a heart of gold will never decay' and today, I was reminded of it again by Madelief."

A few cheers could be heard as people eyed Madelief, some with jealousy while others, like Ida, looked at her with sincere felicitation.

At that moment, the clock began to chime its first chime to signal that it was twelve.

"And so," the second chime went and as the prince spoke, the clocked chimed six more times, "I've decided that the lady that I will marry will be none other than…"

There was a pause for dramatization. The ladies who quietly hoped it would be their names that would be called let out tiny squeals of excitement.

"…Ida Lehrer!" this time, with the eighth chime.

"Ida? How could that four-eyed freak triumph over me? Where is she?" Ida heard Evalia's voice screaming, then some shouts by the prince to have Evalia taken away. However, all Ida saw was darkness as her legs began to wobble as if they were made of jelly and soon she passed out…

"Ida! Wake up!" was what Prince Jesper heard after he had his guards stop Evalia. He rushed his way through the thick of the commotion to find the old lady he had saved yesterday, only this time, much older and lying motionless in the arms of an older Professor Lehrer.

Prince Jesper hurried to Ida's side and tapped her on her face, gently but purposefully, but she did not stir. An orange glow was coming from his pocket and he quickly took out the piece of paper to see it slowly turning into stone.

Prince Jesper did not know what else to do and, in a moment of pure impulse, kissed Ida on the lips.

The soft gasps of many in the crowd culminated into a loud one as thoughts of *Prince Jesper had really become insane* ran through most of their minds.

The king was the only one brave enough to voice it, "My son, have you gone out of your mind? First you chose an old woman to be your bride and now you're kissing her corpse!" Then he motioned to the guards, "Guards, get the prince away from that dead body!"

The prince did not struggle as he was pulled up from Ida by the guards. He stared at Ida's body, as lifelessly as it was staring back at him.

Then, he felt a sensation in his right hand and looked down.

The parts of the paper that had become stones were glowing green and turning back to paper. Then when he looked back at Ida, a white glow engulfed her as her aged skin slowly regained its exuberance. The blondish hair was streaking into red.

This time the gasps were even more profound. The guards were dumbfounded by what had just happened and Prince Jesper effortlessly freed himself from them, running over to be at Ida's side.

"Ida, it's you! It really has been you all along!"

"What happened?" asked a dazed Ida.

At that, Professor knelt down beside them and said, "It would seem that by kissing Ida, you have professed that she would be your wife, turning her into a royalty, hence, freeing her from the curse!"

It was at this moment that Prince Jesper and Ida noticed that the Professor was back to his original age as well.

"Father! Look at you! You're back to your original age again!" exclaimed Ida.

The king, really baffled by the whole episode, decided to speak up. "What's going on here? Can someone please explain to me what magic this is?"

"Father," the prince turned and kneeled before the king, "This is Ida Lehrer who was placed under a horrible curse which is now broken and she shall be my bride."

The king, though still rather confused by all these, decided it was best not to ruin the celebratory mood and declared, "Well then, I believe we have a wedding to prepare!"

To that, everyone cheered.

Happily Ever After

fter the ball, Ida could scarcely remember what had happened as she was no longer the librarian just like how the curse had erased every memory that Prince Jesper had of Ida. However, Prince Jesper was able to remember who Ida was by having pieced together the different clues.

To save them from their agony of this missing part of their memory, I-J decided to throw caution into the wind and explained everything about the Library of Mystory to them. However, they felt it would complicate matters if others knew about this library and its curse so they devised a story about some evil witch from a faraway kingdom who had set a curse on a fine young lady to prevent the prince from marrying her. It was lucky for this fine lady that the way to break the curse was a true love's kiss, the one given by the prince.

Most people readily bought the story and even used it to scare their own children, should they misbehave, that they would be sent off to be turned old by the witch.

The king and queen believed the story of course. They grew really fond of her kind and caring nature and were amazed by the knowledge she had on almost everything! The queen often teased her son that it was his kind fortune to have found such a sincere and intelligent girl.

Ida managed to get Corrina into the castle to be her own lady-in-waiting. Corrina finally got her chance to prove to her old mistress that she was more than 'just a barmaid' and sincerely seemed more cheerful these days.

As for Evalia, she did not take defeat well and nearly went insane. She was housed in the castle for a few days to be attended to by the royal doctors and during those days, Prince Jesper arranged for Kegan to pay special visits to her. Eventually, they both fell in love with each other and were grateful to Prince Jesper for playing the cupid. They planned to get married right after the prince's wedding.

Madelief became close friends with Ida and she went on to graduate with top honours, especially since Ida could no longer go to college to compete with her; the king absolutely would not hear of it, for fear that the 'evil witch' would strike again. Hence, Ida shared many study tips with her, hoping that she would achieve success in Ida's stead.

Professor Lehrer, now considered somewhat a royalty himself, could no longer hold the title of the Head Librarian and so he had to transfer it to the head master, who seemed more than happy to add another 'Head' position to his résumé.

As for I-J, he did not stay for the wedding. The curse did not reverse on him as he did not become a royalty. Since he had reclaimed the missing page that he had come to retrieve, he decided it was best to spend the rest of his shortened life doing what he loved best: sorting books and eating the pages that fell out of them.

Finally, as for Princess Ida and Prince Jesper, they went on to have a blissful marriage and the country prospered under them. And thus, you can say, they lived happily ever after...